For Adam

CONTENTS

1. THE STORM.................................1

2. PIROSKA...............................18

3. PITCH.................................36

4. IREZUMI..............................61

5. THE BOY IN THE BOAT..................80

6. NATURE..............................101

7. MUD.................................129

8. THE MONKEY..........................159

9. THE SCRIMSHAW IMP...................190

10. THE BLACK SHIP.....................212

11. WOLFSBANE..........................231

BONUS STORIES

12. FATHER.............................247

13. THE MERMAID........................252

THE STORM

For three long days the coast had been savaged by
a wild and rabid storm. The waves threw themselves at the ancient cliffs with a rage few had ever
witnessed, and certainly nothing I could remember
seeing in my thirteen years of life – and I had lived
nowhere else.

The Old Inn, my home, squatted on the clifftop,
holding on for dear life like a limpet clinging to a
rock at high tide. It stood on a gnarled promontory
that had been gnawed relentlessly over the cen-
turies so that only a thin trackway connected it to
the rest of Cornwall. It was eaten away on either

side like the core of an apple, undermined to form a bridge and in danger of being bitten clean through and making an island of the inn and islanders of me and my family.

The storm was a killing storm and had raced across the Atlantic without warning, like some wild, ravenous beast. Fishermen all along the coast were caught in its claws and their wan-faced widows haunted the quays and harbour mouths.

On the first day, a clipper that had tried to out-run the storm had been broken up on the teeth of the rocks a mile or so offshore and gone down with all hands, the sea too mountainous for the lifeboat men to reach them.

The day after, another ship, an ancient-looking vessel, had been sighted in the bay, only just visible amid the low clouds and sea spray, and the folk along the shore prayed that it had found some way to outwit the winds and escape the fate of the drowned brig. I did likewise as I stood in the wind-wrecked garden, looking out to sea.

Despite its isolated and precarious location, the Old Inn had always been a popular and friendly place, and much of this was due to my father, who was never too busy to listen to another man's woes or share a joke or dispense some of the wisdom that comes with a vocation such as innkeeper.

Though some may feel an inn to be a less than perfect place for a child to grow up, Cathy and I would not have traded places with any other children in England.

The seafaring men who came to the inn were like our own family. There were those who could be bad-tempered or gruff, it is true, but we could always find someone who would be willing to tell us tales of their adventures and travels. We would sit, spellbound, until our mother shooed us away to bed, deaf to our pleas to stay for just a few more minutes.

No children ever had more love than we did; the memory of it is like a bright light, so intense I can hardly bear to look. But it was not to last.

After our mother died during childbirth, taking our little brother (as would have been) to heaven with her, our father, who had always been the very best of fathers and the noblest of men, slowly slid into a trough of despair, medicating himself liberally with brandy and port and whatever open bottle was at hand.

He had no call for jokes and no man's woes were equal to his own. The wisdom he had gifted others seemed spent. He was sullen and ill-tempered, even to the friends who tried in vain to encourage him to see that he should take comfort in the lives of his children.

But Cathy and I were no comfort at all; far from it. We were reminders of the love he had lost. Cathy was a perfect miniature of our mother and it often seemed to pain him to look at her. Yet no matter how he spurned us, he was still our father and we loved him dearly. He was my model for manhood; I had grown up wanting nothing but to be like him in every way.

Our customers were not so forgiving, however. Gradually the inn began to empty. Long-standing patrons and family friends who had once thought nothing of trudging up the cliff path now stayed in the village, and any passing travellers rode on, forewarned of my father's inhospitable nature.

His mental state grew worse and worse. He flew into uncontrollable rages from which Cathy and I would hide, cowering in our rooms until we felt it safe to come out, invariably finding our poor father drunkenly sobbing to himself in front of the fire. It began to seem as if whatever ties had bound us to him, our father was drifting away from us day by day, staring past us, unwilling or unable to hold our gaze, pushing us away, crying out for a quietude that seemed forever lost to him, and therefore lost to us too.

The storm seemed to be an especially malevolent influence on him. It was as if three days of gales had shaken my father's wits, uprooting and splintering them. He had become oddly invigorated by the wildness of the weather and his actions became more and more excitable and intense.

I observed him from my bedroom window in the cottage garden my mother had lovingly kept but which now was overgrown with thistles and weeds, beaten almost flat by the gales. He was leaning into the wind, harvesting tall blue flowers manically yet methodically, gathering up a sad bouquet. I was shocked to see that he was crying profusely as he did so. It pained my heart to see it.

Then, on the third night of the storm, Cathy and I were struck down by a terrible illness. It hit Cathy first, but only by about an hour. It came on with frightful speed, with strange numbness about the face and throat, followed by the most terrible sickness and vomiting. We were both sure we would die and we called out as we would have done as tiny children, calls that would have brought our mother running up the stairs.

With this crisis my father seemed to come to his

senses. He was like a changed man. He comforted us as dearly as any parent could and said that all would soon be well: he would go to fetch the doctor and we were to stay in the house and on no account leave or let anyone enter. I had never seen him so distraught. He seemed half crazed with worry and we loved him for it.

We promised and he left, assuring us that he would be back before we knew it. My father had placed Cathy and I in his own bed, and we lay there together in the dark. I could hear Cathy's breathing – which, like my own, had become so very fast – gradually slow and calm. Then I fell asleep.

I cannot say how long I slept. The wind around the house was like a dragon's mighty roaring and, understandably I suppose, my sleep was troubled, for I woke into the darkness gasping for breath, like a sailor breaking the surface of a black ocean whose depths had swallowed his ship. But to my great relief, the pains had gone.

'Cathy,' I whispered, 'are you awake?'

'Yes,' she said after a pause. 'But I feel strange.'

I knew what she meant. The symptoms of the illness seemed to have passed, but they had been replaced by an odd light-headedness. I said that perhaps we should get up and wait for Father downstairs by the fire, and Cathy agreed.

We got dressed and made our way down to the main room of the inn, which until recent times would have been filled with the talk of men and the clink of glasses and clatter of pewter pots, but was now empty, the only movement being the jittery, nervous shadows of chairs, flickering in the firelight.

I asked Cathy if she would like me to read to her and she said she would, so we settled down by the fire as we often did. I had intended to read her some childish works of fancy, some frivolous entertainments to calm her in Father's absence. But I should have known better.

Ever since I could remember, Cathy and I had both had the most insatiable taste for stories of a macabre persuasion, particularly those whose plots sailed upon storm-tossed oceans or hauled up on strange deserted shores. It was a taste acquired from listening to the seafaring tales of the regulars at the inn, tales that made little concession to our tender years and would have caused our mother to send us to bed even earlier had she known.

These stories, though gruesome, were as much a comfort to us in their familiarity as a nursery rhyme might be to another child, and it was to

these tales we turned in the hope of being transported from our present woes and worries. They took us back to that happy time when all was well at the inn, a time when death and sorrow were confined to stories and the lives of others.

The wind was so loud about the house and made such moans and mournful howls in the chimney that I had to raise my voice to a most unnatural level to ensure that Cathy could hear me, but she made no complaint and merely sat in rapt attentiveness, hanging on my every word.

'A *scene of the most horrible butchery ensued,*' I read. '*The bound seamen were dragged to the gangway. Here the cook stood with an axe, striking each victim on the head as he was forced over the side of the vessel by the other mutineers . . .*'

The fearsome gale had been tugging at the barn door and slamming it shut repeatedly for an hour or more, and so it was a little while before we registered that the booming we were now hearing was not that sound, but someone pounding at the front door.

I ran to have a look, assuming it to be my returning father. The main door to the inn stood at the end of a small and gloomy stone-flagged hallway and had a round window of thick glass, like that at the end of a bottle. Even in outline I could see it was not Father.

'Hallo there!' said the man outside. 'Will you let a poor sailor bide out the storm?'

'We're closed', was all I could think to say, mindful of Father's warning to let no one in and to stay in the house until he returned.

'Have pity, lad', the stranger shouted above the storm's din, clearly divining my adolescence from my nervous voice. 'All I ask is safe harbour for a while and then I'll be gone. You would not leave a man to die in this foul weather now, would you?'

At these words the roar of the tempest rose to another level of wildness. It did seem cruel to let even a stranger spend another minute in that storm. The wind was so strong it had lifted a barrow and hurled it into the sea only moments before he'd arrived. It could do the same with a man, of that I was in no doubt. Whatever Father had said before he left, I was sure he would let the man in himself were he here.

When I lifted the latch it was all I could do to prevent myself being pinned to the wall by the violence of the opening door, and the roar of the storm and the sea crashing at the cliffs was such an assault on my senses that it took me a while to fully register the figure standing in the doorway, a flash of lightning throwing him into inky silhouette and almost seeming to shine through him in its intensity.

I could not detect any features – he remained a shadow in the doorway – but something in his face twinkled like a tiny star.

'I'll be no trouble nor harm to you or your kin, you have my word.'

Another crack of thunder exploded overhead and I could not in all conscience have closed that door on anyone on such a night.

'Aye,' I said reluctantly. 'Come in, come in.'

'You're a good lad,' said the stranger with a smile. 'Jonah Thackeray doesn't forget a good turn. Pleased to meet you.'

'Ethan Matthews,' I said, taking the hand he had offered and finding it as cold and wet as a fishmonger's. He was comprehensively soaked, water dripping from him as readily as though he had just climbed from the sea.

'Come in,' I said. 'You'll catch your death out there.'

'I thank you kindly,' he said, stepping over the threshold, and I put my shoulder to the door and, after a struggle on the stone flags, managed to get it closed and bolted against the storm. The relative peace once the door was shut was marvellous to behold and our little house seemed more comforting as a shelter than it had before.

When I turned to face the stranger I was surprised to discover that he could not have been very much older than I was – seventeen or eighteen at most. He was dressed in the uniform of a midshipman (though hatless and in a somewhat old-fashioned style), with a black topcoat with brass buttons and a white waistcoat and white shirt beneath. A sword hung from his hip.

There was a black silk neckerchief around his throat and the face above was handsome: dark eyes, like those of a seabird, set in a pale face and framed all about by jet-black hair that snaked downward in shining wet locks. A gold tooth glinted in his broad white smile. Catherine came and stood by me, peering round at him.

'And who might this rare beauty be?' he said. Cathy blushed and hid her face.

'This is my sister, sir,' I said a little stiffly, not overly keen to hear her spoken to in such a forward manner. 'Catherine is her name.'

'Though everyone calls me Cathy,' said my sister.

'I'm very pleased to meet you, Miss Cathy,' said

the sailor, as he gave her a shallow bow.

'Pleased to meet you too, sir,' said Cathy with what I took to be a curtsey.

'But are you all alone here?' asked Thackeray, looking past us.

I felt my hand clench into a fist, suspicious of this line of questioning. Thackeray noted it and smiled.

'Come now, friend,' he said. 'Stand down. I was only asking. Is your mother here perhaps?'

'Our mother is long dead, sir,' said Cathy. 'Ethan and I have been awful sick and Father has gone to fetch the doctor.'

'Cathy!' I hissed, annoyed that she should be so free with a total stranger.

'Well,' she sniffed, 'Father told you not to let anyone in and you have. So there!'

I could hardly argue with this accusation and felt my cheeks burn. The wind roared like an angry beast and seemed to hammer at the door as if trying to gain entrance. The visitor looked at us both with such a strange expression.

'It's a rough night out there,' said Thackeray. 'Has your father been long?'

'Yes,' said Cathy. 'He's been an awful long time, hasn't he, Ethan?'

Again I glared at Cathy for her infuriating habit of saying more than was strictly necessary.

'He will be back in no time, sir', I said, 'rest assured. We are expecting him at any moment.'

'Are you?' he said in a tone I did not care for.

'Yes, indeed', I replied.

'I am mighty pleased to hear it, young fellow', said Thackeray. 'In the meantime perhaps I might have a sip of rum and share your company.'

He took a purse out of his pocket, shook some coins into his hand and emptied them noisily on to the counter.

'I am sure my father would not want us to send you out until the storm eases, sir', I said, looking at the coins. 'You may help yourself to rum. There is a bottle on the counter. Cathy shall fetch you a glass.'

We all three sat down at a table near the fire, Cathy and me at one side, Thackeray at the other. There was a pile of books on the table and our visitor picked them up, reading the titles out loud with a wry smile.

'*Narrative of the Most Extraordinary and Distressing Shipwreck of the Whale-Ship* Essex, *The Narrative of Arthur Gordon Pym of Nantucket, Tales of the Grotesque and the Arabesque* – these are deep waters for ones so young.'

'Do you not like Mr Poe?' said Cathy.

'I like him well enough', he replied, 'though he can be a mite elaborate for my tastes.' He grinned. 'I found The Tell-Tale Heart very amusing – wonderfully gruesome.'

Cathy smiled at this unusual pairing of words, clearly seeing a kindred spirit in Thackeray. I was more wary.

'You are a reader, then, Mr Thackeray?' I asked with a marked tone of surprise. He smiled.

'When I have the opportunity', he replied. 'But we sailors are more likely to tell a tale than read one. It is part of the life of a ship, even a ship such as mine.'

He looked into the fire for a moment, seemingly lost in his own thoughts. I wondered what he had meant by that.

'You have not yet told us how you come to be out on a night like this', I asked.

'I used to live not far from here', he said. 'But that was long ago . . .'

Once again Thackeray seemed to drift off into his own world, and I looked at Cathy, regretting my soft-heartedness at letting this stranger in through the door. We knew most people hereabouts and I knew of no Thackerays. But Cathy seemed spellbound as our visitor turned to face her.

'I was sweet on a girl and would have wed her.' He smiled weakly at Cathy. 'But she married another. I married the sea instead.' He took a swig of rum and looked into the fire again. I rolled my eyes at Cathy and she slapped me on the arm.

'Perhaps,' he said, looking back at us, 'and I only say perhaps – perhaps I might while away some time, as I drink my drink and wait for the storm to quieten, by sharing with you a few tales I've gathered on my travels. How might that be?'

Cathy readily and excitedly agreed that that would be an excellent notion, providing that our guest would not find it too tiring. I mumbled something to the effect that whatever Cathy wanted was fine by me, though in truth I did not want to give this stranger any excuse to tarry.

'My only concern,' said Thackeray, 'is that my tales are too shocking for your tastes. I am used to the company of seafaring folk and our stories have a tendency to be – how shall I say? – of a more bloodthirsty nature than those you may have heard before.'

Cathy and I exchanged glances and I knew that she felt the same as I.

'I assure you, sir, that my sister and I are quite

equipped to deal with anything you tell us. We are not babes. We have been brought up in an inn and we are well used to the ways of seafarers like yourself.'

Thackeray rubbed his hands together and they creaked like old leather. He grinned and his gold tooth twinkled like the evening star in the twilight at the edge of the fireglow.

'Very well, then, young listeners', he said, 'I shall have to think . . . Ah yes. I think I have one you might find diverting. It is a romance of sorts.'

'A romance?' said Cathy with a curl of her lip. She had a spirited aversion to romances of any kind. I smiled at how swiftly Thackeray seemed to have lost my sister's interest.

'Yes', he said, *'of sorts . . .'*

Piroska

Ships can carry many cargoes: opium or cocoa beans, oranges or timber, cotton or cast iron. They have carried invading armies; they have carried slaves. But the cargo the *Dolphin* carried, though human, was of a very different kind.

For a ship can also carry dreams, and the *Dolphin* carried emigrants from the Eastern Mediterranean bound for a new life in America. It carried their physical bodies, their rough clothes, their meagre possessions, but it also carried their hopes and aspirations. And it carried their fears.

These people were not the travelling kind. For

generations their families had clung to the tough lives that had been handed down to them – peasants eking out a living in the shadow of ancient castles. They were a deep and superstitious people, whose fierce attachment to the land of their ancestors had been hard to break.

And so the passengers had boarded the ship with great excitement, had sung folk songs and danced on the deck to the amusement of the crew. The lilting music of fiddles and clarinets filled the air and the ship quickly gained the atmosphere of a country wedding or a May fair.

One of the passengers in particular soon caught the eye of a young sailor called Richard Stiles as he went about his duties: a girl – a red-haired girl – who seemed to glow like an ember, lighting up all those around her. He fell in love in a fluttering heartbeat, though he was too shy to do anything more than smile at her.

There was something childlike about these emigrants. It was as if they were smothering their fears and doubts about the new life under a blanket of merriment and high spirits, as if their songs and laughter were charms against misfortune.

But things changed as they headed out into the Atlantic. A storm crashed into the ship and drove the passengers below deck. Songs were replaced by prayers, laughter by groans and tears. Wives clung to husbands, children to their mothers.

By the time the wind finally dropped a few days later, the emigrants seemed beaten, as if the storm had broken their spirits. The singing stopped, no one danced any more, and even the play of the children seemed half-hearted and muted.

Richard Stiles looked down at the grim gathering below him as he made a repair to the mainsail rigging. He could see the emigrants were mostly from poor stock: farmers and artisans – the kind of people Richard himself originally hailed from. He was reminded of why he had run away to sea in the first place, four years ago at the tender age of eleven; he was reminded of the grey, tedious drudgery of the northern market town in which he'd been born. He understood the passengers' desire to seek out a better life, but they reminded him of his own escape from a life that had almost sucked him dry.

To Richard these people looked as though half their lives had already been spent in the effort of getting this far; they seemed worn away and utterly lacking in any zest for life. It was as if the enthusiasm they had shown at the start of the voyage was like a memory of joy, not joy itself; that it was an act, a sham. Perhaps this was their true form.

'What a cargo', said a sailor nearby. 'You'd think they were going to their funerals rather than starting new lives. They give me the shivers.'

Richard knew what he meant. There *was* something unsettling about this new dour mood. He heard the captain voice concerns to the ship's surgeon that there might be some kind of sickness among the passengers and told the crew that they were to keep their distance.

But unfortunately this strange dullness and sloth had already seeped into the very fabric of the vessel and infected the crew, for they seemed to have adjusted their normal lusty rhythm of life to the mournful tune of their passengers.

Where usually the crew would sing as they worked and share a joke or two, or play some harmless prank to while away the hours, they now went about their duties with the relentless monotony of factory workers. For the first time since he went to sea, life was grim and mechanical, and Richard could not wait to unload these dreary people.

And dreariness of action and temperament was exactly mirrored in their outward appearance. The emigrants evidently did not possess a single item that was not grey or brown or black in colour, and any colour that the ship possessed seemed to drain away in the general gloom of the weather, which had been overcast and dark as a winter's dusk for days.

A fine mizzle fell and the horizon was hidden by low cloud and mist. The sea joined in the general sluggishness, as did the wind, which blew only gently, like an old man's shallow breathing at the end of his days.

But amid this dreary twilit monotone there was one note of joy, like birdsong in a cemetery: the red-headed girl Richard had fallen for. She, at least, had not lost her excitement or joyful vigour. He saw her moving gaily among the lumpen mass of passengers: a deer skipping through a winter forest.

She was slight of figure, and yet brimming with life, her face round and rosy-cheeked, creased by dimples. Her hair was as red as the maple trees of Massachusetts on a bright October morning. Her smile shone like a sun in that gloom and it lifted Richard's heart just to see it.

Of course it was true that the crew had been thoroughly warned against fraternising with the passengers, and though they were ordered to be courteous, Richard knew that he was risking a reprimand even speaking to the girl. Yet speak to her he must.

Disregarding his fears of contracting some sort of sickness, he found an excuse to work on deck among the passengers, and as he coiled a rope he looked surreptitiously about him for a glimpse of her. Then, all of a sudden, she was standing next to him.

'Hello, miss', he said.

When she did not reply immediately he thought that perhaps she did not understand, but then she cocked her head to one side and smiled.

'Hello', she said with a strong accent.

Richard had not prepared a speech and, having found the girl, he did not really know what to say to her. They were surrounded by her fellow emigrants, who, though apparently oblivious to them, nonetheless made him feel self-conscious. She saw his discomfort and giggled.

'You might ask me my name', she said with a teasing smile.

'Do you mock me, miss?' said Richard, the colour rising to his face.

'No', she said sweetly, touching his arm. 'I promise I do not.'

'Well then.' He looked round nervously to see if any of the crew was nearby. 'What is your name, miss?'

'Piroska,' she said.

'That's a beautiful name,' said Richard.

'You think so?' And she giggled again.

'Yes, I do,' he said, embarrassed that she might think he was trying to flatter her when it was simply his honest opinion. It *was* a beautiful name.

'Are you looking forward to living in America, miss?'

'Piroska, please. Yes,' she said. 'I am dreaming of America every day.'

'Your family is with you?'

'Oh yes,' she said. 'Many family are with me now.'

Richard found that he was no longer listening to the words, only watching the movement of the cherry red lips that spoke them. Piroska saw it too, and laughed a warm laugh that Richard could not help but join in with. He felt as though he had walked into a pool of warm sunshine in a dark forest.

'I must get back to work,' he said, 'else I will be in trouble.' He tugged at his cap and began to move away, bumping clumsily into one of the other passengers.

'But you have not told me *your* name,' called Piroska.

He turned round.

'Richard. My name's Richard.'

'Then we will talk again, Richard?'

'Yes, miss – Pir-os-ka. We will.'

And so they did; at first in stolen moments, with Richard forever looking over his shoulder for any sign of the captain or first mate, but gradually, as the days went by, becoming bolder. The strict regulations of the ship seemed to have fallen prey to the same air of lethargy as the passengers and, for this at least, the young sailor was grateful.

Richard was a diligent lad and always made sure that none could reproach him in terms of the work he did, but when he had any free time he spent it with Piroska, and they sat like two lighted candles, aflame with a youthful passion for life.

They would talk for hours and Richard marvelled at how at ease he felt in her company. He had always been awkward around girls, not knowing what to say or how to act. But it was different with Piroska. Despite the fact that they came from such different cultures, he already felt more comfortable with her than he did with his crewmates.

Any shyness he had suffered from, Piroska had cured. No one had ever seemed so interested in him. He talked about things he had never spoken of with anyone, and voiced hopes and ambitions he had not even realised he had until she coaxed them out of him. But time and again he came away from a conversation realising that he still knew almost nothing about his red-haired angel.

'Your family do not mind that I speak to you alone like this, without a chaperone?' asked Richard one day. He had been meaning to ask this for a long time but had held back for fear of hearing or even suggesting some problem.

Piroska smiled and shook her head.

'No, no,' she said. 'My family like you. They are happy that I know you. They would like you to come to America with us.'

At first Richard thought he must have misheard. He had a tendency to gloss over any mention of America, as to talk of their destination and their parting was too painful. He was amazed. He was not even aware which of the passengers *were* Piroska's family and began to feel a little guilty about his lack of curiosity now that he knew of their approval of him.

'Really?' he said. 'I am flattered, but, Piroska, I am a sailor. That is my life ...'

Piroska smiled.

'You will come to America with us,' she said. It was a statement, not a question. He felt suddenly intimidated by her unequivocal tone.

'I must get back to work,' he said.

She smiled and ran her fingers through her long red hair, making it flicker like a flame. Richard watched the light run down its length and stream over her shoulders, and he felt as though he were flowing down with it, as if he were falling help-lessly over a waterfall. It took an effort of will to wrench himself away.

Richard spent the rest of the day in torment. The sea was his home and he had always loved the life of a mariner. Could he really give that up for the unknown trials of a settler? What did he know about farming or shop-keeping? What did he know about anything except rope and sailcloth, knots and rigging?

And yet, much as he loved sailing, he loved Piroska with a different kind of heat and energy. He may once have had a passion for his work, but that was fading now and he wondered if it had ever been as fervent as the passion he now had for this girl.

All through the hours of that day, he found it almost impossible to think of anything else. He nearly fell down an open hatch, he was so preoccu-pied, and as his heart skipped a beat at the thought of the broken bones he would have suffered, he noted that no one around him even seemed to have noticed and would certainly not have had the presence of mind to prevent him. It was as though the whole ship were sleepwalking.

And in a way that helped to make up his mind. The sea and the life of a sailor had been a source of excitement to him, but he could not make any such claim now. He did not fear change any more; he wanted to embrace it.

The fact was he might never again meet a girl like Piroska. She was the most important thing in his life now, by far. He would never have believed that anyone could compete with the ocean for his attentions and emerge the victor, but Piroska had. She was a full moon, eclipsing everything.

It was as if all doubt evaporated in an instant. Everything seemed crystal clear to him now. Whatever new challenges lay ahead in the wild expanses of America, whatever hardships or dangers, he was equal to them so long as he had Piroska by his side.

The sun had set and eight bells rang to signal the end of the last dogwatch. It had been raining steadily all day and the sails hung limply, like giant sheets on a washing line. Every rope and chain and piece of wood or canvas was slick with water and dripped on to the sodden deck.

Richard was soaked through himself, but that did not dampen his spirits as he moved through the lantern-lit huddles of passengers, looking for Piroska. Then, suddenly, there she was, more beautiful, more alive than ever. Richard felt as though they were the only beings truly alive in their small part of the universe.

'Piroska', he said, 'I want to come to America with you, if you still want that.'

'Of course', she said with a smile. 'I am very happy.'

Richard had so much he wanted to say that the words seem to trip over themselves in their eagerness to escape, and he floundered, tongue-tied. He reached out and took her hand in his and was amazed at how warm it felt in the chill of the night and the cold rain's incessant patter.

'There's more', he said at last. 'I don't just want to leave this ship and go to America with your people. I want to go with you. There's something special between us. You do feel that, don't you?'

'Oh yes', she said, her green eyes sparkling with a diamond brightness and clarity. Rain trickled down Piroska's face but she did not seem to care and smiled on regardless. A drop of water ran from her forehead, down the edge of her nose and across her lips. As it left her mouth and dribbled down her chin, it turned red. Richard had seen consumption before and his heart sank as if it had been turned to lead. He remembered the surgeon's talk of sickness.

'Piroska,' he said. 'My love, you are not well.'

'You called me your love,' she said as the trickle of blood dripped from her chin. A tear mingled with the rain on Richard's cheek.

'Yes,' he said, his voice faltering. 'Do you love me?'

'Of course,' said Piroska. 'That is why I have saved you till last.'

Richard frowned, puzzled by what she could mean. The chatter of the passengers and the work of the crew had come to a halt, and Richard looked around to find that the whole ship was staring at him in silence.

The only sound was the gentle whisper of the waves against the hull and the creak and squeak of wet ropes and sailcloth. Richard had a falling feeling, a gut-churning unease. It was as if he were in a dream, though he knew he was awake. Every eye was turned upon him, every mouth was closed, like an audience waiting for the start of a play.

He realised that he had never really looked at these other emigrants since they first boarded the ship. Apart from Piroska they were just an amorphous mass, a single dull entity.

But now he could see their faces, pale and hungry. He saw their limpid, red-rimmed eyes. He saw the livid, ugly pairs of puncture marks that studded their scrawny necks.

When he turned back to Piroska, beautiful Piroska, her smile widened; it widened more than Richard could ever have thought possible. He just had time to register the sharp fangs – and then, with snake-like speed, she struck.

When I looked at Cathy her face bore an expression I knew well: one that was a curious compound of fear and enjoyment. It was an expression that I always hoped to see on ending a story, for it was as sure a sign of satisfaction as a round of applause. Thackeray could see that too, and allowed himself a rather unpleasant smirk.

'Was my story to your liking?' he asked.

'Oh yes', said Cathy, holding her hand to her heart as if trying to steady its beat. 'At first I was a little worried it was going to be some sort of awful love story.' Cathy screwed up her face as if she had tasted something especially unsavoury.

'Well,' said Thackeray, taking a sip of rum and licking his lips, 'it whiled away a few minutes.'

He grinned at Cathy in a most inappropriate way.

'You never did explain how you came to be here,' I said. 'And on a night such as this. You say you used to live hereabouts. I know of no Thackerays in the village.'

The stern and suspicious tone of my voice seemed to amuse Thackeray and he chuckled to himself. But he made no reply all the same.

'Do you have family nearby?' I persisted.

'None that's living,' he said.

'Then why –'

'Is it the one whom you loved you've come to see?' asked my sister.

'Cathy,' I said. 'That's none of your business.'

Thackeray smiled, but I saw a tear twinkle in his eye.

'No,' he said. 'She's gone too, rest her soul. But it is true that the memory of her drew me here.'

The storm seemed to have abated somewhat while Thackeray had been telling his tale, but it returned now in force. The crashing of the sea against the cliffs sounded so close as to be waves crashing against the hull of a ship.

Indeed, with the raging sea all about us and the roaring gale whining round the eaves, it did feel as though we were in the cabin of some storm-tossed brig instead of on dry land. It was an illusion that seemed to please Thackeray. He recovered his good spirits and leaned forward with a wink.

'As the storm has not yet had its fill of us, shall I tell you another tale?'

'Oh yes, please,' said Cathy.

'Ethan?' he asked, looking at me.

'If it will keep my sister entertained,' I said with a shrug, 'then let us hear another. My father may return at any moment and interrupt it –'

At that moment, a cat leapt on to the sill of a nearby window and Cathy and I both flinched, much to Thackeray's amusement. It was the enormous brindled tomcat that was a frequent visitor to the kitchen door of the inn.

'Quite a beast,' said Thackeray. 'Does he belong to you?'

'No,' I said. 'He is a feral cat. Father tolerates him because he says he keeps the vermin down from around the house. He is never allowed inside, but in any case he would not enter. He is wary.'

'Wary?' said Thackeray with a raise of an eyebrow. 'Of what?'

Cathy and I exchanged glances.

'Our father has, on occasion, become . . . *annoyed* with the cat,' I said.

'Your father is a bad-tempered man, then?' said Thackeray.

'He tried to kill him once,' said Cathy. 'More than once. He never normally comes so close, does he, Ethan?'

'Cathy,' I hissed. 'Mr Thackeray does not want to know all our business.' I actually had rather the opposite impression.

'No matter,' said Thackeray with a wave of his hand. 'I was to tell you another tale. Now let me see. Oh yes. I think I have one that may interest you. And it concerns a cat. Would you like to hear it? I am afraid it also involves a murder, Miss Cathy. I assume you have no problem with that?'

'Oh no,' said Cathy eagerly.

'Excellent,' said Thackeray. 'Then let us begin . . .'

PITCH

Billy Harper had a tattoo of a death's head on the back of his left hand – a grinning skull etched into his leathery skin. It was the hand he used for killing, or so he said, and, true or not, it put the fear of the devil in the hearts of the youngest of the *Lion's* crew and most gave him a wide berth.

Harper did not appear especially formidable; he was no more than sixteen years of age and not particularly tall or thickset, or in any way the sort of figure you might mark out as fearsome from a distance. But he had soul-piercing wolf's eyes and a gaze that few could hold, and men twice his age kept a cautious distance. Some people give off a scent of danger that the wise know and avoid and that the foolish are drawn to; so it was with Billy Harper.

Already at this young age he was a drinker and prone to unpredictable moods, as changeable as the Bay of Biscay, with storms to match. One moment he would be laughing and joking, and the next he would lash out at any poor lad whose misfortune it was to be near at hand.

What little gentleness he possessed seemed reserved for Pitch, the coal-black ship's cat. It was strange to see a youth such as he, one so full of anger and darkness, with that cat on his lap, stroking his fur and feeding him scraps of his own food. The cat, for his part, was just as devoted to Harper and would follow him about as he worked, purring and mewing all the while.

The only *human* aboard the ship that Harper seemed to have any affection for at all was a young lad called Tom Webster, though Tom never understood why, for he was as wary of Harper as the next man – maybe the more so for his paying him so much attention. Tom felt as if he were forever sitting on a keg of powder, knowing that at some point it must explode.

And though Tom had done nothing to win Harper's affection, still he was hated for it by his fellows, who shunned him and behaved towards him as if it were Tom himself who treated them so ill, and not Harper.

Tom was as sullen and offhand as he dared be, yet Harper would nevertheless greet him with a grin and a slap on the back, and all about him Tom could sense the cold stares of the crew: Harper was a curse put upon him for a crime he had no knowledge of committing.

Tom feared and resented Harper from the beginning, but these feelings grew over time, distorted and amplified by some growing malady of his mind, until finally Tom hated Harper with a loathing so intense it felt separate from him: almost a living thing in its own right. The violence of his feelings towards Harper were completely out of proportion to the youth's actions and were all the more sinister for being concealed to those around him. He hated Harper and he despised his fellows. He was better than all of them.

That said, Tom had never planned to do it – or so, at least, he told himself afterwards. He was sure that he was not a bad person; leastwise not until that moment. He believed that things just happened to set themselves out that way. Fate lined up the skittles and he had no choice but to knock them down.

After all, had young Tom Webster not been on watch that moonless night, had Harper not stumbled past him, drunk, and leaned over the gunwales – well, then Tom might never have grabbed those legs of his and tipped him over. It was fate, pure and simple. Or so he told himself.

As Harper tumbled overboard, he shot out a hand – that tattooed hand – to grab the rail. Tom stepped back, not knowing whether to help him or not. Some pang of guilt did prick his conscience, but not enough to send him forward. He just stared at that hand and at the death's-head tattoo, twitching and grinning as the tendons flexed and strained.

Then Tom saw that Harper's grip was improving. He could hear him groaning with the effort of hauling himself up. He could hear Harper's feet scrabbling to gain purchase, and now he saw his other hand reaching up to grasp the rail.

That small part of Tom – the wholly good, sane part of him – felt glad of it. But by far the greater part began to imagine what Harper would do to him when he was back on deck. In panic Tom looked about him, and the very first thing that his eyes laid sight on was a heavy hatchet left by the carpenter, embedded in a block of wood nearby.

Without thinking further, Tom ran to where it was and yanked it free. Four or five steps took him back to Harper, whose face had now started to rise above the rail, his expression one of confusion and fury and fear all mixed up together. Tom lifted the hatchet over his head and struck.

Harper had seen the attack coming. His eyes had bulged wide and his mouth opened to cry out, but the sickening blow from the hatchet severed his hand at the wrist and he instantly lost his grip and fell, hitting the water, all sound sucked under like the man himself.

Tom watched for a sign of him among the waves and if he had seen one, he might even have raised the cry of 'Man overboard!' – but the sea had swallowed Harper up greedily. It was as if he had never existed, and though Tom felt a strange feeling in his gut, he could not truthfully have called it guilt or shame; relief was more like it.

The severed hand lay on the deck like some hideous crab, the death's head staring upward. Gagging with revulsion, Tom eased his foot under the thing and flicked it towards one of the nearby drainage holes that pierced the bulwarks, and then he kicked it overboard.

Tom was suddenly horribly aware of being watched and turned slowly to look, fearing that someone had observed his crime. At first he saw nothing at all but the beshadowed ship, then slight movement near the mainmast revealed the source of his uneasiness – Pitch, the ship's cat.

Tom smiled when he saw him. Despite the fact he had never liked the creature – he was associated with Harper in his mind, and was so black as to seem more shadow than flesh and blood – he was so relieved that it was this dumb animal and not a crew member that he could have kissed the cat there and then.

Pitch strolled slowly out into the lamplight and sat looking at him with an expression that seemed to accuse, silently and malevolently.

Had he seen what Tom had done? Had he understood? Tom knew that he should not have concerned himself with such matters, for the cat could hardly peach on him, but there was something about that creature's cold stare that filled him with anger.

Tom moved to chase him away, but before he had taken a step, the cat bolted through his legs and disappeared out of sight into the surrounding

darkness. Tom cursed him under his breath, but he had more pressing concerns.

He quickly cleaned the blood from the rail with water from a nearby pail and threw the hatchet into the sea. Then, with a calmness that surprised him, Tom carried on with his watch as if nothing had happened, and when it came time to be relieved, he took to his bunk and slept easily. Just as the ever-changing sea had closed over Harper, so too had Tom's thoughts; he paid him no mind at all.

The following day the crew were called to attention and told that a man was missing, and that the man was Harper. Tom naturally feigned surprise and joined in with the mutterings and so forth until he realised that Captain Fairlight was standing at his side.

'You were on watch last night, Webster,' said the captain. 'Did you see anything?'

'I did not,' said Tom, all serious and grave and shaking his head. 'Well – that is . . .' he began, with mock confusion.

'Come now, lad,' said the captain. 'Let's hear it, if there's anything to hear.'

'Well, sir,' said Tom, 'I did see Harper at one point. But I don't think I should say . . .'

'Say what, lad?'

Tom took a deep breath and studied his feet for nearly a minute before replying.

'He was drunk, sir', he said, staring at the deck all in sham reluctance. 'And he was still drinking. I told him he ought not to be there but he bade me go to hell, sir, and made to strike me, so I was too afeared to stop him, sir.'

Tom was so taken with his story that he surprised himself when tears sprang to his eyes.

'I know he was not a popular man, sir, but I wish to God now I had been braver so as I could have been some help to the poor wretch. If I had spoken up, then he might still be here, sir.'

Tom flinched as the captain clapped a hand on his shoulder. He feared he had gone too far and given himself away. But the captain was smiling.

'No blame can be laid at your door', he said. 'Not wanting to speak ill of the dead, but Harper was a devil for the grog and, though I like a drop of rum as well as the next man, the sea ain't the place for drunkards.'

There was much nodding and muttering at this, for every man aboard knew it to be true. It was all too easy to imagine Harper had simply fallen overboard in a drunken stupor. Tom could picture it perfectly himself, even though he knew otherwise.

The captain spoke a few words from the Good Book and the crew said their amens. In no time at all they were on with the business of sailing and Harper was lost in their wake. It may seem harsh to those who do not know the sea, but a sailor accepts these things and moves on.

In the days that followed, Tom was surprised to find that some of the crew who had most scorned him for his supposed friendship with Harper now gave him a sympathetic nod and smile and included him in their talk. All the old animosity was gone in an instant. The curse of Harper had been lifted.

The world seemed so much brighter, so much *better* for Harper not being in it that Tom found it hard to believe that his actions could have been wrong. If anything, his death felt like a blessing. In fact it would have been true to say that Tom's thoughts would have been entirely untroubled had it not been for the cat, Pitch.

Tom could no longer, in any degree, bear the company of that creature Harper had held so dear. He had never wasted any affection on the animal and felt the dislike to be mutual, but the cursed feline now seemed to strike a pose whenever he saw Tom, pausing in his cattish activities to look at him in such a way that made the boy feel the cat was judging him.

And how could a cat – *a cat!* – stand in judgement of him, an animal that killed without thought or conscience? Why, Tom had seen that flea-bitten creature kill a thousand times with no more motive than boredom or amusement, torturing some mouse for half an hour before absent-mindedly leaving its headless, uneaten corpse as litter on the deck. How dare this murderous devil judge him? Just because he reserved some special affection for that bully Harper!

It was offensive, and in spite of the fact that none of the crew could possibly know why the cat stared at him so, Tom still vowed that he would not tolerate it. When the opportunity arose, Pitch would join his friend Harper at the bottom of the sea.

The cat seemed to register this change in Tom and, though Tom would still turn to find the animal staring at him from some vantage point or other, as soon as he made the slightest move towards him, the cat would speed away as if the Devil himself was at his tail. Tom had even found the beast peering out of the drain hole through which he had kicked Harper's severed hand. He had come close to doing the same to the wretched cat, but Pitch was too quick for him again.

Tom determined to bide his time. Eventually the cat would let down his guard and Tom would come across him napping on a coil of rope, as he was often wont to do, and then he would see to the animal once and for all. Once. And. For. All.

Later that same week Tom was on deck, lost in these thoughts of how he would do for the cat, when he noticed that the captain and two of the crew were in a huddle near the rail where he had sent Harper to his watery death.

The fear that he was about to be found out hit Tom with such violence that he could barely breathe in that instant and his throat felt as if Harper's ghost had risen up from the deep and gripped him round the neck.

With all his remaining strength Tom approached the captain and the others, sidling towards them so as not to arouse their suspicions. He was disturbed to see that one of the crew was pointing to a nick in the rail, and heard the other say that there was a hatchet missing that had been nearby and this looked for all the world like it had struck the rail.

'And is that blood there?' asked the captain, pointing to the decking under the rail.

'Aye, sir. Blood, sir,' said the sailor, crouching

down and peering at it.

'There's been some evil afoot,' said the captain slowly. 'Say naught for now, mind you, but keep your eyes and ears open.'

Tom cursed himself for a fool. He had cleaned the blood from the rail but had not thought to look at the deck. In any case, it being so dark, he had seen nothing.

But then, of course, he had been distracted by that damn animal too. Had it not been for the cat, he should have thought more clearly. Curse that creature! But it was too soon to panic.

What did they know? Tom thought to himself. They knew nothing. So a hatchet had gone missing and there might be blood on the deck. Harper could have done all that himself. Who knew what a drunk might do? He might have hurt himself and taken the hatchet with him when he fell or jumped. Anything was possible.

And even if they could say it was murder, which they *could not* – not with any certainty – then they manifestly could not say who the murderer was, not with any kind of hanging-proof.

Harper had had more enemies than Judas, as every man aboard knew, and had barely been missed since his disappearance, let alone mourned.

In fact the whole ship knew that Tom alone received kind words from Harper. Tom was the least likely of all to kill him, or so it must seem.

There was no reason to suspect him of anything. It mattered not one jot that the cat seemed fascinated by the scene of the crime – he was not about to speak to anyone. Just the day before, Tom had seen him scrabbling over the side of the ship at that spot and clambering about on the rigging below, where the ropes were fixed to the hull. If only the hated beast had fallen overboard! But the stinking fleabag could stare at Tom as much as he liked – that meant nothing. Nothing!

As if on cue, Tom turned to see Pitch sitting looking at him with his smug and knowing expression, and Tom lashed out with the mop, almost, but not quite, hitting him.

'What have you got against the cat?' said Captain Fairlight, suddenly appearing at his side.

'Against the cat, sir?' said Tom a little nervously. 'Nothing, sir. Why would I?'

The captain grinned and clapped a hand on Tom's back.

'Easy, son,' he said. 'I have no love for that animal either, but he keeps check on the vermin, so he has his uses, eh?'

The captain wandered away. How dull-witted, how simple-minded he was, thought Tom. He shook his head and gave a little chuckle, noticing that he must have chuckled louder than intended, for some sailors nearby turned and stared at him. But Tom paid them no heed. They were all fools too.

Days passed and Tom's mood lightened. The hated Pitch seemed to have disappeared. Tom hoped that some fatal misfortune had overtaken the beast, but would have preferred to see the creature's corpse lying at his feet to know for sure.

If Pitch was not dead, then at least the cat seemed to hold Tom in such dread that he could not bring himself to come up on deck for fear of their meeting, and Tom took pleasure in that.

Tom was working the mainsails one day when he looked down and saw the captain once more studying the rail where the hatchet had relieved Harper of his tattooed hand. Something about the way the captain peered forward and picked at the scar in the wood with the end of his finger made Tom uneasy. Without thinking, he ceased what he was doing and began at once to clamber down the rigging.

But no sooner had he reached the bottom than the captain called to Tom, waving him over, and

Tom wished he had stayed aloft and cursed himself for a fool. He was still muttering to himself as he crossed the deck, but the captain's voice was friendly enough to put a check on Tom's anger and make him come to his senses. There was nothing to link him with the crime other than the fact that he was on watch that night. I *must keep a grip*, he thought. I *must stay calm*.

A sailor nearby looked at Tom strangely as he passed, and he was filled with a sudden panic that he had said these words out loud. He put his hand to his mouth. The captain called him again and Tom hurried over to meet him.

'I need to speak with you a moment, Webster,' he said.

'Aye, sir?' Tom answered. The captain sighed.

''Tis my belief,' he said, dropping his voice to a whisper, 'that Harper did not fall that night – leastwise not of his own foolheadedness – but that he was shoved over.'

'No!' Tom said with all the surprise he could muster.

'Aye,' said the captain, looking about conspiratorially. 'There are signs of evil-doing of some kind. A hatchet has gone missing.'

'A hatchet?' said Tom, shaking his head.

'Are you sure you saw nothing that night, Webster?'

'Quite sure, sir', said Tom. Though he had tried to sound casual, his voice sounded thin and reedy, as if it came from a long way off.

'You're not protecting someone?' the captain said, staring at him in a manner that made him back away and look about nervously.

'No, sir', said Tom.

'This is a bad business, lad. To think there is someone on the ship who has killed. If a man was to know about such a killing and not speak up, he would be as guilty as though he had struck the blow. Are you *sure* you do not wish to tell me something, lad?'

Tom's heart felt as though it was beating so hard and fast the whole crew must hear it. His neckerchief felt as tight as a noose against his windpipe.

'Aye', said Tom, breaking into tears. 'Aye, sir! I do know something.'

'Then sing out, lad', said the captain.

'It was Duncan!' hissed Tom. 'I saw him that night, standing at the gunwales and cleaning something from the handrail. He said he'd kill me if I spoke.'

'Did he now?' said Captain Fairlight, between

clenched teeth.

The blameless Duncan was standing nearby as Tom said these words and instantly pulled a knife from his belt, striding towards him with murderous intent.

'I never spoke a word to you but I'll sure as hell gut you now, you lying swine!' he growled, before he was grabbed and disarmed. Tom had to turn away to hide his smile. The fool was damning himself.

Duncan strenuously protested his innocence, but he had threatened to kill Harper on many occasions and everyone aboard knew he was capable of such an act. Tom smiled again.

'This is no laughing matter,' said the captain, seeing Tom's face.

'Sorry, sir,' said Tom nervously. 'I am just relieved to see him safely held. I was sore afraid of him.' The captain nodded. 'Is he to be hanged?'

Captain Fairlight said that he would lock Duncan up until they got back to Portsmouth, where a judge would decide his fate. He had never yet hanged a man aboard a ship he'd captained and it was a record of which he was proud.

Tom tried not to let his disappointment show. He would much rather have had the man condemned there and then. The more Duncan yelled his innocence, the more men there might be who would believe him.

'I hope you do not doubt my word, sir', said Tom. 'For I would not inform on a man for less than murder, and he'll kill me for sure now if he's released.'

'The law shall decide who is telling the truth, lad', said Captain Fairlight.

'The law?' said Tom. 'It sounds to me as though I am not believed. I must . . .' Tom's eyes were momentarily distracted by a movement beyond the captain's shoulder.

'Calm yourself', said the captain. 'It is not a question of believing you or not believing you. A man's life is at stake here and justice must be done.'

'Justice?' said Tom more loudly than he had intended, and then, seeing the whole crew look round to face him, 'What about justice for Harper?'

His voice crackled with indignation and anger. He looked at their stupid cow-like faces and pitied them for their dull wits. But what was that moving behind them?

'But if he could', Tom shouted, still distracted, craning his neck to try and make out what it was, 'if he could . . .'

Of course! Tom saw that it was the damnable

Pitch, trotting out from hiding at last, no doubt secure in the knowledge that Tom could do nothing while there were so many witnesses.

And then Tom noticed the cat had something in his mouth, and was heading gravely towards Tom as he used to do with Harper when he would ceremoniously present him with a gift of a half-eaten rat or some such.

The cat came ever closer and Tom backed away, tripping over a rope as he did so, mumbling to himself. No one else had noticed the cat, but seeing Tom's wild behaviour, the first mate looked back to find the cause of it – and saw what Tom had seen.

'Captain!' he said. 'Look!' He pointed to the cat, just as that creature opened his mouth and dropped Harper's hand, death's-head tattoo and all, on to the bleached deck.

Tom stared in horror and disbelief. He had kicked the hand overboard. How could it be here? Then he remembered seeing Pitch clambering over the side of the ship. The hand must have got lodged somehow behind the rigging on the ship's hull. The cat – that damnable cat – must have retrieved it!

'Saints preserve us!' said the captain.

The hand had dropped into an attitude as if it was pointing, its index finger jabbing right at Tom.

'T'ain't true!' he yelled. 'That cat is a devil, I tell you. I should have killed him as well when I had the chance.'

'As *well?*' repeated the captain.

Tom looked about him in the eerie stillness that followed – the creak of hemp ropes and the sound of the sea as the *Lion* cut through the waves the only music.

'As well, you say?' said the captain.

Tom stared, his mouth moving but no words emerging, and the crew stared back at him, grim-faced to a man, like the crowd at the foot of a gallows. Then he shrieked with rage and threw himself at the cat.

Three crewmen wrestled him to the ground and he fell heavily to the deck, his face squashed up against the weathered boards, his eyes almost touching the blue-white flesh of Billy Harper's hand and the grinning death's-head tattoo.

Cathy looked at me with wide eyes and I reached out a hand to comfort her. Her skin felt cold to the touch and she pulled away, clearly embarrassed that I should be mollycoddling her in front of this stranger. We were not unused to such tales, as I have said, but this youth had a way of telling the story that made it seem real somehow.

'There now,' said Thackeray, looking at us both in turn with his head bent to one side. 'I wonder if I haven't frightened you both. You'll have to forgive me. I'm not used to telling tales for children.'

There was something about the tone he used when saying the word 'children' that I took offence to. It was true that I was young, but age has more to do with experience than the number of years you may have walked the earth. I was hardly a child. Since our mother died and our father had taken to drink, I had almost run the inn myself and been both father and mother to Cathy. I had listened to the stories of drunks and eased them to the door at the end of the evening. I had been forced to use my cudgel on more than one occasion.

'I cannot speak for Cathy,' I said boldly, 'but though I enjoyed your tale and you told it well enough, my sleep will not be troubled.'

'Nor mine,' added Cathy.

Thackeray nodded and grinned, taking another sip of his rum and sighing.

'That's good drinking rum,' he said. He leaned

back and seemed lost in his own thoughts for a moment.

'You seem a little young to be drinking spirits', I said pointedly.

'You seem a little young to be telling me', he answered with a smile his eyes did not accompany. 'I would have thought you'd be used to the sight of a drinking man.'

'I was brought up in an inn, it's true', I said, 'but it's left me with a low opinion of drunkards.'

'And your father?' said Thackeray. 'Does he have this same low opinion?'

'You must ask him yourself when he returns', I said.

'I would do so gladly', he replied.

I had the distinct impression that he was insinuating something, but I let it pass. After all, how could he be? He did not know my father. He did not know us. I strongly suspected he had never even been in this vicinity before and that everything he had told us to the contrary was, like his stories, pure fantasy.

Cathy had inherited my mother's need to be a peacemaker and leaned between us with a smile.

'I see that you have a tattoo yourself', she said, pointing to the tattoo of an eye Thackeray had on the back of his own hand, an eye with rays of light streaming from it. He looked at it, nodding.

'An old gypsy woman did that for me when I was ten or eleven', he said, smiling at the reminiscence. 'Said it would protect me from harm.'

Thackeray slapped the table, making both Cathy and me jump, and laughed uproariously. I feared he was already intoxicated and my expression clearly gave this thought away.

'I'm not drunk yet, Ethan', he said. 'I was laughing at something amusing, that's all.'

I noticed, however, that he no longer looked in the least part amused, and instead stared away into the middle distance as if entranced. Then, suddenly, he snapped out of it and turned to us, smiling.

'But this is nothing compared to some tattoos', he said. 'This is a child's doodling. I've seen men with pictures that would grace the finest galleries etched into their flesh, with colours as bold as any fresco or altarpiece.'

His smile became a little lopsided and he stroked his chin with his long fingers. 'As a matter of fact, that puts me in mind of another tale I heard once.'

'Tell us', said Cathy. 'Please.'

Thackeray looked at me as if asking my permission.

'Of course', I said, not altogether succeeding in feigning a lack of interest on my part. 'If Cathy would like to hear it.'

Thackeray's smile broadened into a wolfish grin.

'Very well, then . . .'

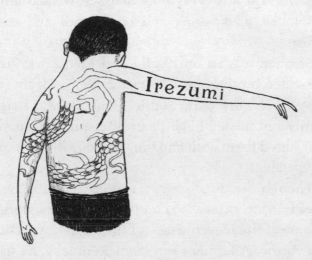

Irezumi

Stephen Fletcher was not quite twelve years old when he stepped ashore in the port of Nagasaki on the island Kyushu in Japan with his shipmate Mattie, gazing in spellbound wonderment at a myriad exotic sights. He marvelled at the people: their strange hair and clothes, and the long swords some carried that Mattie told him could slice a man in two so clean he did not feel the blow until he fell in pieces.

Mattie Husk had taken Stephen under his wing and looked after him aboard ship. He had taught him who to charm and who to avoid, and had no doubt saved the younger lad a beating or two in this way. He was everything Stephen wished himself to be, all swagger and confidence and easy charm.

Stephen was an only child and Mattie was like the elder brother he had never had and always craved. For his part, Mattie came from a large family and missed his little brothers. It was a trade that suited them both and they had quickly become inseparable.

Though he was only seventeen, Mattie was already widely travelled and full of exciting stories – some of them even true – of his many voyages in the Pacific. A farmer's son from Kentucky, he had never even seen the sea until he was ten, when he ran away to seek his fortune. Not that a stranger would ever have known that. He had the air of someone born to the sailing life and always seemed even more at home than Stephen, whose father and brothers had all been mariners.

In fact, thought Stephen as they walked away from the quayside, Mattie was one of those people who seemed at ease in any situation – even in a place as exotic as Japan. He had been to these islands before and clearly enjoyed the idea of being Stephen's guide.

They were walking along a busy side street, when Mattie suddenly announced that what they ought to do most speedily was to get themselves a tattoo.

'A tattoo?' said Stephen warily, for he had been bred to equate tattoos with rogues and ne'er-do-wells.

'Aye', said Mattie, slapping Stephen on the shoulder. 'Every mariner must have himself a tattoo, Stephen, and they do none better than in these parts.'

Stephen was not at all convinced that every sailor *did* have to have a tattoo and was sure that he had seen many aboard their ship without one, but it was part of the machinery of their relationship that Stephen tried to go along wherever Mattie led him, and so he merely nodded, though with little enthusiasm.

'I seen a man once', Mattie said, his eyes bright with excitement, 'a mariner who hailed from these parts and had gone to sea on account of how he'd killed a man. Best part of his whole body was painted over save for his face. It took five years to finish it, so he said. Even them parts most precious to a man was covered.'

And here Mattie winced at the thought of such a

thing, then laughed and said it must hurt like hell-fire and laughed again. But all that did was fill Stephen with dread about the whole notion of having a tattoo as he did not take pain well. But he did not want to show his fear to this lad whose good opinion meant so much to him.

Stephen's sense of unease was not helped by the fact that they had now set off into the backstreets of that place, deeper and deeper into a darkening maze of shops and alleyways. Mattie had a piece of paper that he would occasionally take out and consult, but it was clear that he was lost. Stephen was about to point this out, when they noticed an old man smoking a long pipe outside a dingy-looking building.

'Horishi?' said Mattie. 'Irezumi?'

It seemed like the fellow had not heard Mattie at first, or at least not understood him, for there was a long pause while he inhaled another heavy swig of tobacco smoke and then, without looking at Stephen or Mattie or the building he sat in front of, he waved a finger at the door and they took that as their invitation to enter.

Inside they found a large room, the walls of which looked like tattooed skin, covered as they were with all manner of coloured prints of demons

and dragons and so on. It made Stephen's flesh
itch.

A flickering red lantern gave a kind of movement to these painted monsters and made them
seem to shimmer and twitch and shudder; sweat
began to bead on Stephen's forehead – and he could
see the same was true of Mattie, however tough he
talked.

It was so dark that it was a little while before
they realised that anyone else was there. In fact
Stephen started and gave a gasp as a man loomed
slowly out of the shadows and asked them in
English what they wanted.

'Irezumi', Mattie said again, which by now
Stephen guessed must mean tattoo, and the man
nodded and waved his hand around at the surrounding pictures, inviting them to choose a
design. Stephen's eyes were more drawn to the collection of spikes and needles and sharpened
bamboo that was laid out on a nearby table.

Mattie walked up to the walls and then turned to
him, grinning.

'Look at these', he said excitedly. 'I'm going to
have me one of these here dragons on my back.
How about you?'

'I don't know', Stephen said. 'I ain't sure, Mattie.'

Mattie chuckled. 'You ain't afeared now, are you, Stephen?'

Stephen's blushes were hidden by the all-embracing red glow from the lantern.

'I didn't say that,' he said defensively, if not quite convincingly. 'I just don't want one today.'

'That's fine by me, Stevie,' said Mattie good-humouredly. 'Next time, eh?'

'Aye,' said Stephen. 'Next time.'

All the while, their host was watching these exchanges with a smile of indeterminate emotion, a smile that made Stephen even more uneasy about the whole venture.

The man nodded and led Mattie back to the table, where Mattie took off his jacket and shirt. Stephen was so unnerved by the whole atmosphere of the place that he almost decided to wait outside in the street, but he could not bring himself to leave Mattie with this sinister man.

For he had assumed that this man was the tattooist, and was surprised when a curtain was suddenly pulled back and a beautiful woman stepped out from an adjoining room, her face as white as chalk, her lips blood red, her hair long and black and sleek as polished jet.

She wore a long white silk gown that flowed on

to the floor like milk and hid her feet, so that as she moved towards Mattie, she appeared to slide like a ghost. She led him to a kind of padded table where she bade him lie face down. With a small bow to Stephen she pulled a fine mesh curtain to screen them off, though she was still palely visible.

Stephen was left with the man, who smiled his curious and disturbing smile and stared at him fixedly. In an effort to ignore him, Stephen's attention wandered to the paintings on the wall and to one in particular: an image of some sort of demon with bulging eyes and flaming hair and tusk-like fangs for teeth. He held a chain on which there seemed to be a row of collars, like dog collars, or the restraints that might be used on slaves or prisoners.

'You like?' said the man, who had appeared at Stephen's side with unnerving stealth. It seemed such a curious question to ask about such an image that Stephen was caught off guard.

'Yes . . . it's very good,' he mumbled. 'Very realistic.'

The room had become very hot all of a sudden, and airless with it. Stephen sat down on a stool and leaned back against the wall. The room seemed to be throbbing, and the throbbing was echoed in an intense headache that had come upon him suddenly. He decided to close his eyes a moment, but no sooner had he done so than Mattie was already standing in front of him, shirt on and ready to go. He got up, eager to leave.

Stephen was amazed at how quickly the tattoo had been done. The beautiful tattooist stepped back and bowed like a theatre performer, and walking backwards, head lowered, disappeared once more behind the curtain as silently as she had entered.

Mattie thanked the man whose role was still unclear to Stephen, and he bowed in return to both of them. They emerged from the tattoo den in a daze. It was only once they were walking away into the raucous clamour of the city that Stephen realised no money had actually changed hands.

They returned to their ship, the *Charlotte*, with barely a word said on the way, and went straight to their hammocks. Mattie seemed sullen and tense and Stephen knew from experience that when Mattie was in such a mood it was best to leave him be.

Thoughts of the strange tattooing den, the sinister owner, the beautiful tattooist, the demon on the wall, all crowded together in Stephen's mind and meant that it was a little while before he fell into a fitful sleep, but by the time he awoke the following morning, the whole event seemed more dream than anything else.

The *Charlotte* was already heading away from Nagasaki and Japan for the islands of Hawaii when Stephen stepped out on deck. He was happy to be sailing once more. Mysterious as the ocean was, he felt at home there and content. Though the *Charlotte* had a moody and petty captain with a bully for a first mate, still Stephen would rather have been at sea than ashore.

Stephen knew the same was true of Mattie, and sought him out, assuming he would have returned to his usual self. But Mattie's mood had not improved. Whenever Stephen tried to speak to him, he received only a grunt in response and Mattie seemed to find any excuse to move away from him as soon as possible. It was as if Stephen had done something to offend him, though he could not think what that might possibly be.

These concerns were set aside, however, when a sudden storm blew up and threatened to take them all to the bottom of the sea. Despite the ineffectual ranting of their captain, the crew saved the ship with the loss of only one of their number.

But the storm's passing did not bring a return to normality between Stephen and Mattie. Pride conquered Stephen's sense of hurt and eventually he stopped even trying to make conversation with his friend. Whatever the reason was in Mattie's mind for his coldness towards him, Stephen was sure he had done no wrong and he was damned if he would beg for his attention.

They went about their work like strangers. When Stephen noticed Mattie at all it was with a cool detachment. He was surprised to notice that though the weather was fine and the work as hard as always, Mattie did not strip to his trousers as was his normal habit, but kept both his shirt and jacket on at all times. He had thought that Mattie would have taken every opportunity to brag about his new tattoo and exhibit it to the crew.

Thought of the tattoo took Stephen unwillingly back to Japan. Whatever it was that had changed things between him and Mattie had begun there somehow, that night in Nagasaki. Stephen wished they had never stepped ashore, or at least never stepped into that foul place, but it was done now.

Mattie was like a different person and not just in the way he behaved towards Stephen. Where once he had been all life and confidence, he was now edgy and apprehensive. It troubled Stephen whenever he thought of it, but there was a lot to do on the ship, with much to distract him, and it worried him less and less with each passing day.

The *Charlotte*'s captain continued his sullen and petty ways, and so it was no surprise when two of the crew deserted on Hawaii, though Stephen was saddened that one of them, a boy about his own age with whom he had become quite friendly in recent days, had said nothing to him by way of farewell.

The *Charlotte* sailed on over the wide Pacific with a fair wind at her stern. In no time at all the bay of San Francisco opened up before them, and Stephen had already decided that when they moored he would look to join a new ship.

Mattie had done everything in his power to avoid him on the crossing, but Stephen felt in spite of that, for old time's sake, he would seek him out and say goodbye before he left. He had to search the entire ship before he found Mattie skulking about in the darkness of the hold.

'What do you want?' said Mattie in a brittle, anxious voice, his body visibly flinching at Stephen's approach.

'I'm leaving the ship,' said Stephen, trying hard not to let Mattie's hardness affect him. 'I just thought I would say farewell.'

Stephen stepped forward to shake him by the

hand, but Mattie backed away, wild-eyed.

'Stay away', he hissed, looking round madly, his eyes bulging and glistening like fish eyes.

Stephen did not know what to say. He had accepted that he and Mattie had drifted apart, but to hear such a bald statement finally brought the tears to his eyes.

'What is the matter with you?' shouted Stephen. 'Ever since that night in Nagasaki you have changed. I wish to God we had never gone to that vile place.'

'Aye!' said Mattie passionately, tears in his eyes too. 'It's my own self that's to blame. But how could I have known?'

'Known what?' said Stephen. 'What ails you?'

Mattie winced and groaned and turned to look at Stephen with a face so changed it shocked him: a face now pale and drawn, with eyes so sunken as to be almost beyond recognition.

'What is it, for God's sake?' said Stephen. 'What is the matter?'

'Do you not know?' he said. 'Do you honestly not know?'

Stephen's mouth became dry. The image of the demon in the tattoo den in Nagasaki stole into his mind and glowed with such luminescence that it was as if it were there in front of him.

'The tattoo,' said Stephen. 'My God, Mattie; is it the tattoo? Show me your back, Mattie. Show me!'

'My back?' said Mattie. 'You want to see *my* back?'

'Aye!' said Stephen.

'But there's nothing on *my* back to see,' said Mattie. 'Don't you remember?'

Stephen stared at him, utterly confused.

'I was about to have my tattoo done,' continued Mattie, 'when all of a sudden you burst in like you were possessed and demanded you had yours done first.'

'Mine?' said Stephen. 'But I have no tattoo.'

'Oh, but you do,' said Mattie. 'And a fearful thing it is. A great demon with blazing eyes. And her that did it just seemed to touch your back with the colours, and they seeped in just where they needed to be. It was magic, Stevie – sorcery. When I saw her do that, I changed my mind about getting that dragon done and we left after you came out of the strange mood you were in.'

'What nonsense is this?' shouted Stephen. 'I'd know if I had a tattoo, wouldn't I?'

'Well, it's there on your back, Stevie.' Mattie looked at the floor and shook his head. 'And I seen it move.'

'What?'

'I seen it move, damn you!' said Mattie, looking up at him with glistening eyes. 'Now stay away!'

'You're insane!' said Stephen, ripping off his shirt and turning his back to Mattie. 'I have no tattoo! Look!'

Stephen expected some response, but there was only silence. When he turned round again, Mattie had pinned himself against the far wall, more crazed than ever.

'Sweet Jesus,' he muttered. 'Oh God. Oh sweet Jesus.'

'What is it?' said Stephen. 'Have you gone completely –'

Then Stephen saw something move out of the corner of his eye; he felt it too, like the draft from a breeze or the feeling of sunlight striking bare flesh when the clouds part. Even so, it was a few seconds before he realised *what* was moving.

Looking down at his own bared torso, he saw something flicker across it, like a shoal of colourful fish. It disappeared round his left side and reappeared under his right arm.

Stephen grabbed at it with his hands, trying to wipe it off. But it was not crawling over his flesh; it was swimming across the surface. It was part of his flesh. It was a tattoo: a moving tattoo. It was the demon Stephen had seen on the wall of the dreaded den in Nagasaki.

'Help me, Mattie!' cried Stephen.

But Mattie was shaking with fear, pointing to the tattoo as it swam round once more. The collars on the chain the demon carried were no longer empty. Three men now swung by their necks, screaming silently in torment: the man they thought had been washed overboard in the storm and the two who had supposedly deserted.

The demon ceased its giddying movements and settled on Stephen's chest, where it rose, expanding all the time, its arms becoming Stephen's arms, its terrible flame-eyes and fang-toothed face becoming Stephen's. Mattie screamed but it was a silent scream, as he joined his shipmates on the chain of the demon tattoo.

Thackeray stared right at me when he had finished, as if challenging me to show any fear. But I refused to give him that satisfaction, regardless of the disquietude he had invoked and the drum of my cantering heart. It was Cathy who spoke first, her voice a little breathless.

'You know so many stories,' she said. 'Are you a writer, Mr Thackeray?'

'A writer?' said Thackeray with a grin. 'Me? No, no, Miss Cathy. I am a sailor, nothing more.'

'Then how do you come by such tales?' I said. 'Who makes them up if it is not you?'

'It is a tradition aboard our ship that the men tell each other stories to while away the long sea hours. Sailors live a life at the edge of humanity, not quite a part of it, not quite removed. It is a world of shadows and shifting light, like the ocean itself. It is this world that spawns such stories.'

The wind moaned plaintively in the chimney nearby.

'You talk as if these tales might be true,' I said.

Thackeray made no reply. He picked up his glass, but paused before it met his lips.

'Come now,' I said. 'We may be young but we are not fools.'

'The sea is a world that no man truly knows, however much he might make that claim,' Thackeray said after a pause. 'It is constantly changing, constantly moving. It is a living thing, never ageing, but never the same.

'There are things abroad on the ocean, swimming in its murky depths, afloat on its shimmering surface, that are not recorded in the pages of any books. They are spoken of in hushed voices, passed from ship to ship, from mariner to mariner.'

'But surely –' I began.

Thackeray raised his hand to interrupt. 'You are a sceptic, Ethan. I respect that.'

'I think I know the difference between a story and the real world,' I said.

'Do you now?' he said. 'Then you are a wise man.'

I did not much care for his tone and hoped my expression told him so, but as usual he merely smiled.

'And you, Miss Cathy?' he asked, turning to my sister. 'What about you?'

'Well . . .' said Cathy, biting her lip and glancing at me. 'Ethan is perhaps more certain of things than I am. I know I am probably foolish, but I rather hope that there are such wonders in the world. I think the world needs wonders.' She blushed and giggled. 'Even awful ones.'

'That's all very well, Cath,' I said, 'but –'

'Shall I tell you of another such wonder?' said Thackeray, ignoring me and looking at my sister with a most unpleasant grin. 'Of another such *awful* wonder?'

'Yes . . . please', said Cathy nervously, her blushes fading instantly.

'Very well, then', he said.

Thackeray glanced at me, as if inviting an objection, but I shrugged and bade him continue.

The Boy in the Boat

The *Roebuck* was three days out of Fortaventura, sailing west. It had taken a beating in the Bay of Biscay and had done some running repairs in the Canaries before heading to the Bahamas with a hold full of supplies for the colonists in the West Indies.

Davy Longman was in his favourite place, perched up high in the crow's nest, searching the wide horizon. The captain had told him to keep a special lookout for ships, because it was well known that pirates infested these waters.

Davy was often given this job, his young eyes

being sharper than most. He would look back and forth across the ocean, and only when he caught sight of something he thought of interest did he raise the telescope.

And so it was this time, when Davy's keen eyes spied a shape on the waves some two miles ahead. He did not call out, because even at that distance he could tell it was not a pirate ship.

With the telescope to his eyes he could see that the object was a small boat, floating alone in the wide ocean, and Davy quickly scanned the horizon for sign of ship or land or possibly wreckage that might explain where it had come from, but there was only a great expanse of water and naught else.

The ocean was in a mellow mood, but even so the boat rose and fell dramatically, disappearing from view every few seconds behind the waves. It was not for a little while that Davy realised there was anyone aboard, and when he did, he could scarcely believe what the telescope revealed. He clambered down the rigging as fast as he was able.

'It's a boy, Captain,' said Davy when he reached the quarterdeck all breathless. 'There's a small boy in a boat up ahead.'

Sure enough, as the *Roebuck* approached and manoeuvred itself alongside the little boat, there was the lad, looking up at Davy and the rest of the crew, barely eight years old.

On the captain's orders, men climbed down the hull and brought the boy aboard, then fixed a line to his boat and hauled that aboard likewise. The boy said nothing when questioned and the captain hoped that they might garner some clue from the boat as to where he had come from.

But the boat was such an odd-looking craft – too small to be a lifeboat or launch. It looked more suited to a boating lake than the ocean, and on its prow on either side, instead of a name, there was a curious painting of an eye.

As for the boy himself, never had Davy seen a more serious-looking lad; though perhaps that was hardly surprising given his situation and having been lost at sea alone at such a tender age. He had a mop of blond hair like ripe wheat and a face so grave it would melt the heart of even the coldest customs man. Davy wondered that the boy had not burst into tears in fear or relief, or in memory of whatever terrible predicament had resulted in him being cast adrift upon the ocean.

The captain, who was a kind and gentle fellow, attempted again to ask the boy what had happened, but he made no reply, looking in turn from one crew member to the other with his big glistening eyes.

The first mate wondered aloud if the boy was perhaps not English and did not understand the captain's question, and so the captain began again in French, but with a similar lack of response.

As everyone knows, a ship's crew is like an island of all nations and the Roebuck was no exception. They had a Spaniard, who spoke his own language and a little Portuguese, an Irishman and a Pole. When their efforts failed the captain even let the cabin boy try in what little he could remember of his own mother-tongue from before he was sold on the slaving coast of Africa. But still there was no response.

Davy, along with everyone aboard, felt sure that this poor lad must be the sole survivor of some devastating wreck or storm-forced sinking and that the circumstances of this event must have been so traumatic that the boy remained in shock. Whatever the cause, the effect of this fragile little survivor on the crew was remarkable.

There were men aboard the Roebuck who would think nothing of stabbing a fellow crewman in the liver with a marlinspike if they were crossed, but Davy marvelled at how these same seasoned mariners now doted on this little boy as though he were their own child, so eager were they to make him smile; but to no avail.

Eventually the captain bade the men go back to their work and let the boy have some space to settle himself, and said that the poor lad might speak when he recovered from his shock. The boy looked from face to face with the same mournful expression as the crew reluctantly backed away and then he wandered over towards the ship's carpenter.

Ludlow was a great bear of a man, his face half hidden by a wild black beard, who seemed to prefer the company of his tools to other men and saved all his affections for wood.

But just as with the rest of the crew, the carpenter's weathered and seasoned heart was mellowed by the sight of the young passenger and he gladly suffered him to come and watch him work – something that would have earned Davy or any of the other men a grunted curse.

Ludlow was repairing a section of the gunwales. Davy noticed that the boy seemed to study the actions of the carpenter with intense concentration. His eyes seemed to glow with a curious fascination at every movement of the man's hands, until something extraordinary happened: the boy smiled.

The carpenter was using a chisel to make a mortis joint when he glanced up and saw the boy's face, and he was entranced by this change of expression; it was like the sun coming out on an overcast day. His lapse in concentration had painful consequences, however; the blade skittered across the surface of the wood and struck his hand, gouging into the flesh at the base of his thumb.

Not surprisingly, Ludlow swore profusely, throwing down the chisel and clutching his torn and bleeding hand. He hissed and winced with pain and cursed his own stupidity.

There was nothing remarkable in this. All carpenters are wont to injure themselves from time to time and Ludlow's reaction was that of any man in similar circumstances. No, the remarkable thing – the thing that caused Davy and every man among the crew to cease their own work and stare in the carpenter's direction – was not *his* behaviour at all. The remarkable thing was the reaction of the *boy*.

For the lad stood before the carpenter, his head thrown back in laughter as if he were watching a Punch and Judy show. He had not once opened his mouth since coming aboard, and now his boyish laughter rang round the ship like a bell.

It was so clear, so joyful, it sounded as though a

host of angels had come among them. Davy felt it seep into his whole body until his very soul vibrated to its song. After a few seconds every man aboard was laughing too, from the hold to the topsails.

The carpenter frowned both at the boy and then the crew for laughing at his misfortune, but soon even he could not resist the seductive quality of that sound. Even as the blood dripped from Ludlow's hand, he shook his head and laughed along with everyone else.

Davy was astonished to see the rough-tempered carpenter taking the accident and the boy's amusement in such good sport, and it seemed to all the crew that this boy was some joyous spirit, gifted to them by God, and every man felt his heart grow lighter for his being there.

It fell to Davy to look after the lad, since he was – until the boy's unexpected arrival – the youngest of the sailors. The captain bade him see to his welfare and make sure that he came to no harm.

It was not a job that Davy bore well, as it was not in his nature to nursemaid a small child, however much that child delighted the crew. But Davy did as he was told, as all men must aboard a ship at sea.

Wherever the lad went, Davy saw that he was

always greeted by a grin or a chuckle and a ruffle of the hair, and this attention was itself rewarded by a smile: his remarkable, heart-warming smile. The very sun appeared to shine brighter when he smiled and everyone within view had no choice but to stop work and bask in its radiant glow.

Had the boy not been so well loved, the captain would surely have been less forgiving of the disruption he caused wherever he went. Men who were normally steadfast in their work now kept losing their concentration and falling prey to all manner of silly accidents, tripping and blundering around like clowns at a May fair.

But whatever happened and however bruised the heads of those who fell, curses would quickly turn to merriment as the boy opened his mouth and laughed his wind-chime laugh, as if all this was being done for his particular pleasure.

Only the ship's carpenter seemed less than bewitched by the boy's presence, though he laughed as all the rest did. But Davy could see that however much Ludlow held his belly and slapped his thigh, he did not laugh with his eyes. And the boy saw it too.

This lack of enthusiasm did not in any way deter the lad from seeking out the carpenter's company;

far from it. The boy seemed drawn to the man despite the latter's unease. And for his part, Ludlow seemed to become distracted, and in his distraction he became clumsy.

One day, as Davy and his charge walked by, the carpenter was sawing a length of wood. Davy saw beads of perspiration appear on Ludlow's forehead as they approached, as if he were straining to keep his mind fixed on the job in hand, and then the relief when the boy chose to walk by without watching him.

But as Davy followed the boy there was a cry of pain from the carpenter. He turned to find Ludlow clutching his left hand and Davy could see that he must have struck it with the saw. He was moaning and gibbering and fell to his knees, fumbling in the sawdust for something.

Davy was about to take a step towards him when Ludlow picked the thing up. It was his thumb; he had sawn straight through his hand and severed the thumb entirely. As Davy took this in and moved to help the poor wretch, with others of the nearby crew, the boy's laughter suddenly rang out once more.

Every one of them turned in shock towards him. Surely he could not be laughing at a man hacking his own thumb off; young as he was, he should know better than that. Though Davy was charged with the boy's safety, he now strode towards him, fists clenched, not knowing what he intended, save that he wanted to stop that laugh.

And yet Davy had taken not more than two steps when a crewman to his right erupted in laughter. Then another began behind him, and another. Soon Davy could see that every man was trying to stop himself from laughing, with various degrees of success. And Davy was no better: the muscles in his face were pulling back into a grin, and a chuckle was fluttering in his throat like a trapped bird. He seemed to have no choice but to laugh himself.

Worst of all, though, was the sound of the carpenter on his knees, laughing uncontrollably through the pain as he stared in grinning, wide-eyed horror at his severed thumb.

Davy and the whole crew of the *Roebuck* now shared the unease of the poor carpenter. Ludlow had become a shadowy figure, muttering to himself and nursing his bandaged hand, which he would let no one look at. The boy who had seemed such a sweet and fragile ray of sunshine in their lives now revealed himself as some kind of cruel curse.

A Kentish man called Smollet fell overboard, his

leg tangled in a rope that had been tied off to the mizzenmast. The rope stopped his fall three feet short of the sea, but brought him to a halt with a wrench that snapped his leg and then slammed him against the hull again and again until he was hauled on deck, so broken he could not be helped. He died in the night.

Then the Irishman named Connolly, whose cat-like grace on the rigging was the envy of every sailor who saw him, fell while climbing the main channels and broke his neck on one of the ratlines, hanging there like a fly in a web while the boy laughed his golden laugh.

There were times when Davy saw crewmen turn as if they intended to strike the little lad, but as soon as they saw his round angelic face and that sweet laugh tickled their ears, they could no more have harmed him than harmed their own babe.

At length Davy saw the captain in discussion with some of the crew, and when the boy was otherwise occupied the captain told Davy that they must talk without fear of the boy's interruption or without influence from the boy's charm.

He instructed Davy to lead the lad to his cabin, show him inside and then shut the door behind him. He handed over a key with a very serious expression, telling Davy to lock the boy in and join the others on deck.

Davy did as the captain ordered, and the boy seemed oblivious to any trick, walking into the captain's cabin without a care in the world and allowing himself to be locked inside without complaint. Davy expected to hear the boy at least try the door, but he did nothing. Davy joined his fellows gathered about the captain, who called for them to speak freely and to voice whatever views they had about the boy.

'He needs killing,' came the immediate reply from one of the older crew. 'He needs killing, mark my words.'

'You can't kill a little boy for laughing when he ought not,' said the captain. 'We're not heathens!'

'It ain't the laughing and you knows it, with all due respect, sir,' said the man, whose name was Beaker. 'He don't just laugh. It's him what's making those things happen. He's a devil and he needs killing.'

And as he said those words Davy knew there was truth in them, even though he might never have had the strength to admit such a thought to another. He could see that the others knew it too.

'He ain't no more a natural boy than I'm the

Virgin Mary', said Beaker. 'Killing him wouldn't be no crime. Besides, who knows he's here but us?' He slapped his hand against the mast. 'I say we kill him and be done.'

Many of the crew shouted their agreement.

'I'm in charge here!' said the captain. 'I say what happens aboard my ship.'

'Aye, sir', said Beaker gruffly. 'Beggin' your pardon, sir.'

The captain took a deep breath before speaking again, his voice now soft and laced with sadness.

'If I agreed to this course of action, then we would *all* have to agree. We would *all* be murderers, whoever did the deed. Are you game for such a plan?'

'Aye', their voices echoed around the deck after a pause.

The captain swallowed dryly.

'I suppose it should be me who does the killing, then', said the captain. 'I cannot ask a man to put such a stain on their immortal soul.'

'I'll do it, sir', said Beaker. ''Twas my idea. You're a good man, sir, and you ain't got a killer's heart. It won't be my first time in that regard and if I'm going to hell already, which I more than likely am, this ain't going to make no difference.'

The captain nodded grimly, unable to look

Beaker in the eye. 'Very well,' he said, handing him the key. 'But make it swift.'

'Aye, Captain,' said Beaker, already starting towards the door to the cabin.

Beaker unlocked the cabin and Davy could see that the boy was standing in the doorway as if he were waiting for him, and he made no attempt to resist as Beaker grabbed him and pulled him out on to the deck.

The sailors, who had so readily agreed to this course, now seemed rather more reluctant to see the deed done and they shuffled and looked out to sea or at their boots or up into the sails – anywhere but at that boy.

Beaker picked up a length of rope and with practised ease he quickly formed a bowline and tested it a couple of times before turning back towards the boy, who looked at him with fascination.

Beaker took one glance at his crewmates, but it was all they could do to meet his gaze. He picked up the loop and licked his dry lips. But instead of fear, Davy saw that the boy smiled as the noose was placed around his neck.

'Beaker!' cried a man beside Davy. 'Look out!'

One of the big wooden blocks from the main rigging swung through the air on the end of a long rope with enough speed and weight to demolish a wall. Beaker took a step back and grinned as it skimmed past.

But the grin was short-lived, for another block as weighty as the first struck him a glancing blow to the back of the head, spinning him round so that the first block on its return hit him full force in the face, sending him sprawling across the deck, his head cracked open like an egg.

The boy began to laugh his sparkling, magical laugh, and so did Davy and the rest of the crew, even as they stared in horror at Beaker's shattered face, almost unrecognisable as the man who moments before had stood before them. Almost unrecognisable as *any* man.

And as they laughed and gasped at the effort of laughing despite the fear and anger and dread they all felt, the ship suddenly lurched and there was a terrible rending and cracking of timbers, and they knew straightway they had struck some hidden reef or rocks.

The boy seemed untroubled by this state of affairs as the ship tilted and groaned and took on water, and the crew in turn laughed like fools alongside him.

The mainstay snapped like a piece of thread and

the topmast broke free, crashing to the deck to kill four men outright. Those that were left laughed on, though tears ran down their cheeks with the effort of trying not to.

The very ship itself seemed to come alive with ropes coiling themselves round necks and splintered wood jabbing and thrusting through bodies like skewers through meat. The whole fabric of the ship fell down around them, crippling many – Davy included – as it did so; collapsing into the boiling sea and dragging the crew with it.

Davy managed to grab a passing spar and hang on with his one good arm, the cold sea numbing the pain of his broken legs. As his grip started to fail and his face began to slide under the water, he became aware of a sound nearby and he turned his head to see that a boat had survived the wreckage. There was someone aboard. Hope suddenly welling up in his heart, Davy called to the boat, but his excitement was short-lived.

The boat he had seen was the strange craft in which they had found the boy, and it was the boy's face that looked at him now. The boy smiled briefly before his face returned to the same melancholy expression he had worn when the *Roebuck* had picked him up.

The last thing Davy saw as he lost his grip and slid beneath the surface of the sea was the boy in his boat, drifting away from the flotsam of the *Roebuck*, away into the wide expanse of ocean.

A branch swung against a window pane and rattled its twigs across the glass, drumming like impatient skeletal fingers, and Cathy and I both started at the noise. Thackeray leaned back and grinned, but his face suddenly changed to one of sadness.

'Ah, drowning,' he said with a sigh. 'That's a poor death, let me tell you.'

He said these last words with such feeling that I softened a little in my view of him and wondered if he had lost a friend to that fate. The storyteller poured himself another drink and stared at me with a strange penetrating expression that made me shift uneasily in my chair. It infuriated me that this slight youth should make me feel so boyish and immature.

'The night is drawing on,' he said, 'and still there is no sign of your father. I hope no misfortune has befallen him.'

He said this in such an odd way that no man

who heard it could have said he wished my father ill, nor yet could they have said that our guest cared very deeply about his well-being.

'You love your father?' Thackeray said.

'Of course!' I replied. 'What child does not love their father?'

'The frightened child,' he answered. 'The child of a cruel and vicious father.'

I got angrily to my feet, but Thackeray paid no heed and looked at his drink, not at me.

'You have a nerve to come here and be a guest in our house and insult our father!' I shouted.

'I have never met your father, Ethan,' said Thackeray. 'You asked if a child were bound to love its father and I answered. If you see an image of yourself in the answer, don't blame me.'

'I saw no such thing,' I said. Cathy looked at me with tear-filled eyes.

'Then all is well,' said Thackeray.

But I did not like his questions or the way he reminded us about our father's absence, and I wished dearly that I had never let him in, for I knew I would have the devil of a job to get him out. Thackeray seemed to read my mind.

'Perhaps it is time I was on my way,' he said, finishing his drink.

'No', said Cathy. 'The storm is still fierce. We would not hear of it, would we, Ethan?'

'Of course not', I said with little enthusiasm.

Indeed it would have seemed a sin to send someone out into that wild night – even someone as strangely unsettling as Thackeray.

'Do you know any more tales, Mr Thackeray?' said Cathy.

'Aye', he said. 'I have tales aplenty. What kind of story takes your fancy?'

'Do you have any about sea monsters?' said Cathy eagerly, oblivious to the danger I felt emanated from this stranger.

'Sea monsters, is it?' He put his fingertips to his forehead, the tattooed eye on the back of his hand standing in disconcertingly for his hidden eye. 'Let me see now.' I could have sworn here that both real and tattooed eye blinked. 'Well. I do not have a tale about a sea-serpent or a kraken or that sort of thing, but I do have a tale about a fearsome kind of creature that did rise up from the sea and wreak havoc aboard a sailing ship.'

'Was it a giant squid?' said Cathy.

Thackeray shook his head and smiled.

'Not exactly. It's a story about a snail.'

'A snail?' I said with a raised eyebrow. Cathy

looked a little crestfallen and I allowed myself a smirk of satisfaction.

'Well – not just one snail, of course,' he said. 'And not just any snail. But let me tell the story . . .'

George Norton's father was a wealthy man, a naval hero who had successfully turned his considerable energies and military efficiency to the world of commerce, building a trading empire with few rivals. Though George was the youngest of the family and still only fifteen, he felt it entirely reasonable to have expectations.

But George had been a continual disappointment to his father. His two elder brothers seemed to have inherited his father's bravery and bluff common sense, traits that George sadly did not seem to share in any measure. George's interests lay elsewhere.

He was obsessed with the natural world – particularly (because of his own nature) the smaller and humbler species of the animal kingdom – and he already had an extensive collection of invertebrates. He had trays full of beetles and cabinets of moths and butterflies, all pinned to boards with their names written down in George's neat italic script.

He had developed a special interest in snails and had boxes of their shells and page upon page of drawings he had made of the patterns they carried. Indeed his father had once jokingly suggested that George was more interested in 'those damned snails' than he was in his own family. But George had not laughed.

Instead of the dynamic life his brothers imagined for themselves, George fantasised about the life of a country parson, reasoning that such an existence would afford him the time to pursue his studies. He had spent many a happy hour in quiet imagining of this life – the house he would occupy, the wife he would marry, the children he would bounce on his knee and the great leather-bound study of molluscs he would publish to the acclaim of his peers. But George's father would have taken violent exception to such ideas.

Before George knew where he was, his father

was informing him that he had used his considerable influence to get George placed aboard one of the many merchant ships that carried his goods across the globe.

George tearfully begged him to reconsider, explaining in no uncertain terms that a boy of his tender health could not be expected to live such a life. His father's response to this was to laugh loudly and clap him on the back, saying, 'It will be the making of you, lad!'

George had a much more certain presentiment that it would be the death of him and this feeling of approaching doom stayed with him as he was rowed across to his ship – the *Swift* – at anchor in Plymouth Harbour some weeks later. No man ever climbed the scaffold at his execution with more of a sense of dread than George did, climbing aboard that ship.

His first voyage was not a happy one. The *Swift* was several days out of Hispaniola when a storm hit. The captain did all he could and were it not for his skills the ship would surely have gone down with all hands. They lost three men overboard and one who fell from the rigging and snapped his neck. Many others were nursing injuries.

George himself had been laid low during the

storm by violent sea-sickness, exacerbated by the lack of sympathy he was given by his fellow crewman in the sick bay. While the crew had battled valiantly to save the ship, George had cowered in his bunk, hoping to hide the storm out, praying tearfully that he would be among the saved.

And so he was. The ship had been badly mauled though. The mainmast was broken in two and the rudder all but torn away. Sea water had leaked into the holds and spoiled the food stores; kegs and barrels had been smashed and split open and their contents floated in foul pools. All this should not have mattered as they had not been far from port, but with the rudder gone they were drifting aimlessly into unknown waters.

When George was well enough to venture out on to the deck he found the ship in a poor state. The crew were in a foul mood and the cause was not difficult to detect. The ragged sails hung forlornly above them and about them the sea was calm to the horizon and back.

As George walked to the gunwales and looked over the side, he saw that things were worse still. The ship seemed to have become entangled in a huge floating accumulation of weed.

This weed was a sickly green in colour and

seemed so thickly massed that George imagined that he could have stood upon it and it would have borne his weight.

Even as he thought this, a putrid stench rose up from the floating weed – a vile smell that he could not place, save to say that it made him wretch almost instantaneously. Two sailors stood nearby and George expected them to grin at his weakness as they had done so often on the journey, but instead they looked towards the weed with expressions of dread.

George had always taken some heart in the past from the way that whatever difficulty they encountered – storms or shallows – the crew all seemed to take it in their stride, but he shuddered now as it became clear that this was something new, something they feared as much as he. For with the damage wrought to the ship by the storm and the lack of wind, they were imprisoned by this weed. Their food supplies were ruined. They would have to make as many repairs as possible and hope that help came soon.

Attempts were made to free the hull from the encircling mass of vegetation, but to no avail. Men were sent down on the end of ropes, but no amount of hacking at the slimy stems seemed to have the slightest effect on the weed as a whole and the ship remained trapped. All that was left was to pray for a fair wind that would blow them clear, but as yet none was forthcoming.

Then, as George looked back at the weed he noticed something strange sitting on top of it. With a nimbleness and cavalier attitude to his own safety that surprised all who saw it and had witnessed George's fumbling and comical attempts at climbing the rigging, he tied a rope to the rail and, taking a firm hold of it, leapt over the gunwales and clambered down the hull. He managed to lean out and grab the thing and scamper back aboard.

The captain stood amazed.

'I never thought I should live to see the day that you would look anything like a sailor,' he said. 'If you hadn't been your father's son, I would have left you behind at the last port and said good riddance.'

George frowned at the grins of the crew all about him.

'What is it, then?' said the captain. 'What has finally put the wind in your sails?'

George looked from face to face and then slowly held the creature up – by its shell.

'A snail, sir,' said George. 'Some kind of sea-snail. I believe it may be a new species and . . .'

But he never finished his sentence – or rather he did finish, but the tail of it was hidden beneath the laughter from the crew. They slapped their legs, they pointed, they brayed, they turned and walked away.

George pursed his lips and held back the tears that pricked his eyes. He looked at the snail. It was clearly some sort of sea creature, not unlike the common whelk – but of uncommon size. This creature was huge: its shell was the size of a bowling ball, coiling up to a shallow cone, patterned all over with streaks of pale pink and grey.

Unlike the shellfish George had seen so often as a child among the rock pools of the Cornish coast, this creature did not have a watertight hatch to seal it against the sea, but instead seemed more like the land snails he had collected at home.

A sailor walked by and looked at George and chortled.

'Let's have a look at your snail, then, boy,' he said.

George reluctantly held it out. The sailor leaned forward to inspect the squirming body of the exposed creature and could not resist the impulse to reach out and probe its flesh.

The very second his finger touched the creature he cried out in pain and pulled his finger away, cradling it in his other hand and allowing no one near. When the poor fellow finally let others nearby help him, they were shocked to see that the end of his finger had been stripped of its flesh to the first knuckle. Gobbets of blood leaked from the wound and dripped on to the weathered decking.

They turned as one towards George, still holding the sea-snail, whose blood-soaked flesh writhed obscenely. George snapped out of his trance and dropped the thing to the deck, where it righted itself with horrible efficiency and began to slide away, leaving a crimson trail behind it.

The captain had by this time discerned that something was amiss and had stepped down from the quarterdeck to see what was occurring. With a cool speed he looked from the sailor's mauled finger to the horrified faces of the onlookers and then to the escaping creature. He strode forward and stamped his boot heel down upon it with brutal force.

George cried out as the extraordinary shell was smashed, but he had never seen such an awful expression of disgust on a face as when the captain lifted his foot and beheld the vile, ruined thing beneath. It was an expression mirrored in all the faces around him.

For, in truth, the crushed thing amid the shattered remains of its shell seemed less like shellfish and more like something from a butcher's block: more like raw meat or offal.

'Do you see what you've done, you useless lump?' the captain barked hoarsely, then he turned to the crew, telling them to get back to their work. George saw with some satisfaction that the captain walked with unusual haste back to his cabin. The boorish man seemed to have met his match – in a snail.

The injured sailor cursed and bled profusely and the ship's surgeon took him below to complete the work begun by the snail and sever his finger. George alone stared at the crushed sea-snail, marvelling at what an addition it would have made to his collection.

'Clean that vile mess up, Norton,' said the first mate as he walked by.

But what they did not realise then, though it would have made little difference if they had, was that this fearsome sea-snail was not alone – that the mass of weed in which the *Swift* was entangled was home to a whole colony of the creatures.

Gradually, more of the creatures slowly appeared on the deck and George was not the only one to notice that it was the blood from the sailor's ravaged finger and the smeared remains of the squashed snail that seemed to be attracting the newcomers, like nectar calls to a bee.

To George this was fascinating; to the rest of the crew, his fascination was as loathsome as the snails themselves. The first mate had caught him attempting to keep one of the creatures in a box, and the captain said that if he did it again, he would be flogged, father or no father.

At first, as each snail slithered slowly over the gunwales, a sailor would be ordered to pluck the creature off, taking care not to touch the flesh, and it would be tossed over the side. The captain clearly had no wish to see another of them smeared across the deck and neither did anyone else.

However, as more and more of them came aboard, George privately began to wonder whether this method was not simply allowing them to return. He was at the point of voicing this concern when another thought occurred to him, one that might elevate his standing with the crew. In fact, thought George, it might make him a hero.

George spoke to the ship's cook. At first his idea got short shrift, but the more George elaborated, the more the cook began to see that there might be something in what George was saying: that here was a wonderful source of meat. All it took was a quick experiment with a pan of boiling water, and the cook was more than convinced.

The cook spoke to the first mate and met with the same scepticism he had felt himself. But he had prepared the snail and offered it to him to sample. Did the French not eat snails? the cook said. Did the British not eat cockles and mussels and the like?

George walked over just as the cook was getting to the end of his speech, holding out the platter with the snail in the centre, cooked in a little oil and garlic.

The first mate grimaced but the cook laughed and said that it would be a fine revenge on the bloodthirsty devils. On the cook's insistence, the first mate gingerly picked up the meat, sniffed it and then took a reluctant bite. George fully expected him to spit the mouthful across the deck, but instead his furrowed brow lifted in surprise and he began to savour it.

He took no persuasion to have more and agreed readily with the cook that it tasted like some marvellous cross between the meatiest salmon steak and the tenderest piece of lamb imaginable. It looked like the *Swift*'s food worries were over –

they had a seemingly endless supply of meat.

The crew were initially as sceptical as the first mate, but once they too had tasted the meat, all doubts were thrown aside and even the poor man whose finger had been gnawed by one of the creatures was soon chewing heartily upon his attacker's kinfolk.

The captain had been the hardest to persuade. He retched in disgust at the thought of eating the snails, but, like the others, his revulsion disappeared when he was finally persuaded to taste it.

That evening George and the crew sat down to a great feast of snails, with every man eating like a king. The cook had generously given George the credit for the idea of eating the creatures and he was cheered and patted on the back. He had never in his life known acclaim, and it felt good; it felt very good.

They ate until their stomachs could take no more, and for the first time since George left port he went to his cot without even the faintest pang of hunger and fell into a blissfully deep and childishly trouble-free sleep.

That night George dreamed a wonderful and poignant dream in which he was married to the elder of the two Harris daughters from Weymouth, whom he had admired on many an occasion.

In his dream he was the vicar of a country parish and they lived together in an idyllic rectory on the edge of a charmingly picturesque village, where rosy-cheeked simple folk tipped their hats and said 'G'mornin'' to them as he composed his sermon in the shade of an apple tree, his young son and daughter playing merrily in the sunshine.

He was deliberating which text to use as the basis of his sermon, with the Bible open in his lap, when he happened to notice a movement from the corner of his eye.

A nearby rose with swan-white petals was being attacked by a huge snail that was grazing along its stem, biting off leaves and buds, sending them fluttering to the ground.

George was incensed and reached out to grab the snail, but as soon as he did so it bit into his fingers, gnawing at the flesh and sending blood streaming down his arm and splashing across the pages of his Bible. He screamed in agony and woke up.

But the screaming continued.

George woke from his dream like a bear dragged from hibernation. It took him a few moments to even recall exactly where he was and he stumbled about in the darkness, striking his head painfully on a beam.

Another scream sounded out, then another. They seemed to be coming from various parts of the ship, and he could hear the sound of running footsteps on the decks above. One of his fellows came over from the next bunk; the lantern he was carrying illuminated the fear in his eyes.

'What is happening?' he asked.

George's throat was so dry he could not find a voice and so simply shook his head in answer. But then he saw something on the beam behind the boy with the lantern and guessed immediately what the cause of the screams might be.

George pointed and the boy turned to follow his gaze. Making its steady progress along the timber was one of the sea-snails, and as they looked about them they quickly saw that there were many, many others.

As another voice cried out it became horribly clear that while they had slept the creatures had continued to climb aboard, and with only those on watch to check their progress, the creatures had overrun the ship.

Where earlier they had delighted in their numbers when they regarded them as food, this abundance was now nightmarish. Eating the creatures had seemed to curb the crew's fear of them and to mentally reinstate their rightful place in the scheme of things. But now they were once more reminded that as *they* were food to the crew, so the *crew* were food to them. They came aboard with one purpose only – to feed on human flesh.

George and the other lad decided to quit the confines of their berth and go up on deck, where at least they might see more clearly. The sight that met their eyes when they did so was like a scene from hell.

Everywhere there were men with vicious wounds to their arms and faces, men who had awoken to find themselves being eaten alive by the creatures. These men were relatively lucky, however.

Lying partially hidden under a length of canvas near the hatch were two sailors who had suffered the attentions of the bloodthirsty creatures. The snails must have attacked some vital organ or artery, or perhaps induced a fatal shock; whatever the method, these men were plainly dead.

A tearful young lad had been given the task of keeping the swarm of snails from feasting on the corpses. George could perceive a twitching movement under the canvas, which indicated that he had not been entirely successful.

In spite of his exhaustion, the distressed boy pounced on every snail he saw and smashed it with a belaying pin. But though the snails were hindered by speed, they more than made up for this disadvantage by their numbers.

No doubt attracted by the overpowering smell of blood, the snails were swarming over the bulwarks, through the gun ports and up the rigging. Though the entire crew was engaged in a frantic effort to stop them, inevitably they could not stop them all.

As George stood there, dumbfounded, rooted to the spot by fear, he felt a strange sensation in his boot, as if the leather had suddenly sprung a leak. This was immediately followed by sharp pain and he looked down to see with horror that one of the creatures was gnawing into his foot.

George cried and kicked out, but the creature held fast. He could feel it rasping into his toes and had he not had the presence of mind to stamp down upon it with his other foot the thing would have bitten clean through to the bone. As it was, the wound was astonishingly painful and it did not take a deal of intelligence to determine why that should be.

It took all George's nerve to do so, but he managed to pick up the crushed body of the creature that had attacked him, its slimy body glistening horribly free from its shell, and hold it up to a nearby lantern.

Amid the disgusting, offal-like substance of the creature's body, he could clearly see concentric circles of sharp triangular teeth surrounding its mouth. George leaned forward for a closer look, when the teeth suddenly jerked into action, snapping together with horrible speed, as if it were some infernal machine.

George dropped the thing to the deck at once and stamped and stamped with the heel of his boot until there was nothing remaining but a greasy smear of gristle and blood.

A cry suddenly went up that there were men deserting in the lifeboat and George felt a desperate wish that he were among their number. He ran with others to the side and saw the boat pushing off into the weeds, a lantern at their prow and stern.

He longed to be in that boat and would gladly have endured the taunts of his fellows in return for escaping from that hell. But it soon became clear that if there were to be an escape, it would not be by this method.

As the deserting crewmen attempted to row their way through the encircling weed, their oars became so entangled that they could not shift them, though they strained and heaved with all their might. One of their number stood up to gain extra purchase on the oar and there was a crack as it snapped in half at the rowlocks.

The others in the lifeboat berated the man, calling him every low name known to a sailor. He responded by waving the broken oar in the manner of a club and threatening to dent the head of the next man who insulted him. All this was greeted by jeers and catcalls from the crew watching from the *Swift*. After a little time, the man threw the piece of oar down and turned to the ship.

'Throw us a line then, damn you all!'

'The snails can have you!' shouted the first mate. 'It's no more than you deserve, you cowardly scum!'

'For God's sake!' shouted one of the men in the lifeboat. 'Show some mercy!'

'Throw them a line, Matlock,' said the captain.

'But, sir –'

'If we are to die, let's all die together,' he said quietly. 'Throw them a line.'

The word 'die' tolled like a bell in George's mind. Were they really in danger of dying? But of course they were. They were trapped. They could not keep these monsters at bay for ever. Was this how he was to die, unknown and unsung – his passing marked by nothing but a faint ripple in the ocean?

The first mate ordered a line to be thrown, but before the rope reached the side of the ship there was a cry from the boat. One of the deserters stood up, screaming and tugging at his clothes. When he turned we could see the cause: a snail had crawled on to his back as he sat in the boat and had clearly bitten into him halfway up his spine.

One of his fellows grabbed the snail and tried to pull it off, but this merely increased the poor man's torments and he flailed wildly about in his panic, striking the other a blow to the side of the head and knocking him out of the boat.

The man in the sea tried in vain to get back to the lifeboat, but every movement simply served to further ensnare him in the green tentacles of the floating mass of weeds. He stretched out a hand towards the ship, shouting for help, but he was too far away for his friends to pull him aboard. All this was illuminated by the ghastly glow of the boat's swinging lanterns.

Meanwhile more snails had begun to creep on to the lifeboat and the efforts of the men to halt their entry and the wild spasms of the man with the creature gnawing into his back caused the boat to rock violently, and to no one's surprise it soon tipped over, spilling all the remaining men into the weed-choked sea.

A line was thrown from the ship and one of the deserters even managed to grab hold, but no sooner had he done so than he cried out in agony as an unseen snail took hold of his flesh. His screams were echoed by the screams of his fellows as each in turn fell victim to the creatures.

Tears sprang readily to the eyes of the crew who had only minutes ago wished these men would rot in hell. But hell itself could not hold torments worse than those souls underwent, eaten alive by the slimy demons.

George and the others stood and watched in a trance as each man writhed in his death throes and then went limp, held fast by the weed, heads lolling hideously atop the green carpet. It was only when the snails began to slide across the faces of their former comrades that they turned away. No man among them had the stomach for that sight.

It was as if the glut of food brought about by the

sailors' escape attempt had driven the snails into a kind of frenzy of bloodlust. As soon as they moved away from the remains of the lifeboat crew – remains which a quick glance told George were picked to the bone – they renewed their assault on the *Swift*.

They now came in numbers that made their previous attacks seem tame by comparison. There were thousands of them. They slid over the gunwales, over the deck, the rigging, the bones of the fallen. The dreadful ponderousness of their movement only made the invasion more nightmarish.

A sailor who foolishly panicked and sought sanctuary in the crow's nest was simply pursued there by the snails, who slowly and relentlessly attacked him in such numbers that he threw himself off rather than be eaten alive.

He landed with a sickening thud on the deck, where the blood immediately attracted the attention of every snail in the vicinity. Some men moved to try to stop their advance but the captain called to them to halt.

'Better that they feed on him than us,' he said grimly. 'He knows no different.'

Something in George snapped. He did not know what to do, but he could not stand there and watch death inch towards him in this way: to have that slow torture of knowing that the most excruciating end was laboriously approaching.

As the captain called them to the middle of the deck to form a protective circle with lanterns at their centre, George grabbed a lantern too before ducking out of sight and heading below deck. He had to sidestep several snails along the way; they altered course as soon as he passed and set off slowly after him.

George, almost hysterical with fear, threw himself headlong into a cabin and bolted the door behind him. He slumped exhausted on to a bunk and then realised he had not checked for signs of snails and set about doing so with a racing heart, and only when he was positive that he was quite alone did he lie back down on the bunk.

George put hands over his ears to block out the cacophony that throbbed through the fabric of the ship: the terrible distant screams of his crewmates as they eventually succumbed to the army of snails.

Worse still was the dreadful almost-silence that followed, in which the soft slither and rasp of the retreating snails could be heard on the decks above.

It was hours before George built up the courage to even consider stepping outside, and when he

did, the eerie mother-of-pearl light of daybreak was seeping through the open hatch.

As he climbed the ladder to the weather deck above, George slipped on the slimy remains of a snail and cracked his head against the wooden handrail. He allowed himself a wry chuckle as he imagined the irony of having survived the onslaught only to break his neck in a fall.

George was grateful that he could see no sign of living snails, but the results of their passing were everywhere. It was like a battleground. The white bones of the crew lay all around: skeletons picked clean of all flesh so that they looked as though they were the sleeping crew of some ghost ship.

George went to the rail and looked over the side. The weed was gone, completely gone. The ship was free. A breeze ruffled his hair for the first time in days. But what good was it? He could not sail the ship alone. He was little use when there had been a full crew, but alone he was worse than useless. He was destined to drift in the open ocean until starvation or shipwreck did the work he had denied the snails.

Something trickled down George's cheek and putting his hand to his face he realised he was bleeding from the blow to his forehead when he had slipped. A droplet of blood dripped from his hand and fell to the deck, striking the bleached boards with a small crimson splash.

George became aware of a curious sound he could not place at first. It was a hollow rattling and rumbling that seemed to emanate from the very bowels of the ship, and he wondered whether it had drifted towards hidden rocks.

But he soon realised that this was not the case. The sound was not coming from the hull but from the holds, and he saw, emerging from every hatch and hole, a million hungry snails creeping slowly, inexorably forward.

Cathy's face was even paler than before. I am sure I was in no better condition. I had always had an aversion to shellfish of any kind, quickening my step past the whelk and cockle stalls in the market, repelled by both their smell and appearance; it was a revulsion I feared this story would only compound.

'Were you never tempted to go to sea, Ethan?' said Thackeray, sitting back, and running his fingers through his raven hair. 'Being as how you lived so close to her shores all your life and how these rooms have been filled with mariners and their tales, did you never want to venture forth and see what lies beyond that horizon?'

'No,' I lied. For how could I have gone to sea, leaving my father to cope alone and Cathy to deal with his drinking? What right had I to choose that path?

Thackeray nodded and smiled a sad smile that seemed to say that he guessed my thoughts, and though it was a sympathetic smile I still resented it.

'Maybe it is for the best,' he said. 'For the oceans are well stocked with dangers of every species and it is an act of blessed fortune to see through a natural life.'

'It was not cowardice that stopped me, if that's what you think.'

'Oh, do shut up, Ethan,' said Cathy.

'Now then.' Thackery held up his hands to pacify me. 'Don't get yourself so riled. I did not mean to suggest anything of the sort. There are many kinds of bravery. It takes as much courage to bring a child into the world as it does to cross swords or sail into the teeth of a storm – more, maybe. I can see you are no coward, Ethan. No offence meant.'

'None taken,' I said after a pause. 'Forgive me. I have my father's temper.'

'Ah yes', said Thackeray. 'Your father. There is still no sign of him.'

'He will be here soon enough. Never fear.'

'Of course.' Thackeray drained his glass.

'You seem mightily interested in my father's whereabouts', I said, despite Cathy's shushing.

Thackeray smiled.

'I have no interest in your father, I assure you', he said. 'Besides, he might not be so welcoming as you and your fair sister. He has a temper, you say?'

'No more than most men', I lied.

'But what about the cat?' said Thackeray with a mock puzzled expression. 'I thought he almost killed it.'

'Oh, but he was drunk', said Cathy by way of explanation and then clamped her hand over her mouth, realising that she had said too much.

'Cathy!' I said, louder and more roughly than I'd meant. Tears sprang to her eyes.

Thackeray poured himself another drink. I put my arm around my sister. She pushed me away.

'My father is a good man!' I said, turning to the sailor.

Thackeray nodded.

'He can forget that sometimes when he drinks', I continued. 'But at heart he is a good man.'

Something happened, though, in the saying of these words – which were passionately meant. I had the strangest sensation that I no longer believed what I was saying. I searched my mind for happy childhood memories, but my father made no appearance in them. I had convinced myself that drink had changed him, but had he ever been the good father I wanted him to be?

Thackeray ran his fingers through his still-wet hair.

'As I say', he said in a bored voice, 'I do not know the man. Your faith in him does you credit, Ethan. No doubt he is on his way home, safe and sound. But in the meantime shall I tell you another story?'

I opened my mouth to speak, but not quickly enough.

'Oh, I was hoping you would', said Cathy, clapping her hands together.

MUD

Ben and Peter Willis were twin brothers. They had
been brought up on the north Norfolk coast and
knew those creeks and marshes like they knew the
pores and creases of their own grimy skin – skin
that seemed to hold the stain of that mud in its
every crevice.

It felt to Ben that they were tied to one another
by some invisible bond. He could not remember a
time when they had been more than a dozen yards
apart. Peter regularly used the word 'we' when
another person would have used 'I'. He would say
'we're hungry' or 'we're tired' and simply assume

that Ben shared these feelings, which, to Ben's annoyance, he invariably did.

Ben had never felt truly alone. He had never felt that he existed as a single entity, independent from his brother. It was as if it took two of them to make a whole, and, without Peter, he was incomplete: a half-thing.

He had never expressed these concerns to Peter; in fact this secrecy was a form of rebellion, as it had always been assumed that they would share everything. Ben concealed his feelings whenever possible and considered every hidden grievance a small victory over the tyranny of twinhood.

But far from freeing him from these thoughts of being forever bonded to his brother, Ben had become obsessed with the notion that they were two opposing parts of a single personality. He had come to believe that Peter was the corrupt, venal and irksome part of himself, the tainted part of his own soul.

This was not a view that many who knew the twins would have shared. For the truth was that both the brothers were rogues, and if anyone had bothered to try to differentiate the degree of their delinquency, they would certainly have said that it was Ben rather than Peter who seemed the one most lacking in any redeeming qualities. For Peter did at least have charm. Granted, it was a charm that was manufactured at will as a distraction from his true character, much as a stage magician distracts the observer from his sleight of hand, and consisted mainly of an incongruous, dimpled smile, more suited to a choirboy or a gilded cherub, and a disarming honesty about his dishonest ways. But it was a charm that Ben entirely lacked.

Ben saw Peter as the demon on his shoulder who led him reluctantly and unwittingly towards misdeeds and wrongdoings he would otherwise have shunned. He attributed to his brother an almost supernatural ability to tempt and persuade that served as an excuse for his own craven and weak-willed nature.

Every time he stole, or lied, or struck some poor unfortunate with a cudgel or threatened them with the blade of his knife, he let himself believe that he would never have done so without the malevolent influence of his twin. Broken bones or broken promises, it was never his fault.

Peter was fond of smiling his dimpled smile and saying, 'I'm right here, brother. Don't you worry.' When they were small it had been a comfort. Peter had always been the braver, always fearless in his defence of his brother. Now it sounded like a threat, like a life sentence.

Ben and Peter had gone to sea together, sailing aboard the merchant ships that plied their trade between Norfolk and the Low Countries. It had been an escape from a dull and joyless life, but every time a storm engulfed them, Ben reminded himself that this too had been Peter's idea and that left to his own devices he might never have left the relative safety of dry land.

But whatever the truth, the twins were mariners now, and in spite of the dangers the life seemed to suit them well enough. Sailors were not entirely bound – or at least did not *feel* entirely bound – by the same rules as those ashore. The brothers were quick to take advantage of all the 'opportunities' that a sailor's life provided.

Back in their home port of Lynn once more, Ben resentfully told himself that the meeting they were about to have with local smugglers was, again, solely Peter's notion – though Ben's hunger for the promised cash had, if anything, been keener than his brother's.

The smugglers thereabouts were as secretive and mysterious as masons, but the brothers had a con-tact – a childhood friend – who had acted as a go-between. The Willis twins had arranged with

Tubbs, the quartermaster aboard their ship, to load a boat with some of the contents of the hold while the captain was ashore in Lynn, being dined by the mayor.

At the appointed hour the boat was duly loaded and Ben and Peter climbed stealthily aboard and began to row towards the shore. It was late afternoon; the sun was low in the western sky and the sea was as smooth and burnished as a silver platter; the noise of the oars and the call of distant curlew were all that broke the tranquillity of the scene.

This peacefulness was all external in Ben's case, for he had a rising dread of meeting the smugglers; smugglers thought little of murder, especially when it came to boys like him and Peter.

Peter, by contrast, seemed to be positively enjoying himself, grinning from ear to grubby ear.

'Here we are,' he said, stopping rowing for a moment and letting the boat rock to and fro on the grey waters. He cupped his hands around his mouth and made a startling impression of an oyster catcher.

From out of the marshes came the sound of a curlew.

'They're here,' Peter said, rowing once more, and he steered into a narrow creek, hidden from the sea by a mud bank. 'Come on,' he said, tying the boat to an ancient, lichen-encrusted stave and jumping on to the bank.

They covered the merchandise they carried in a rough blanket and pushed the boat into an even narrower channel so that it was entirely hidden from view.

Then Ben found himself, as usual, following Peter into the unknown – up a rough track towards a small tavern, whose flint walls faced out to the sea, bathed in the warm low sunlight. Black smoke coiled from massive chimneys.

Walking into the Black Horse was like walking into a cave, and it took Ben a while to see anything at all. Slowly, out of the gloom, a stone-flagged floor appeared, a low black-beamed ceiling, a dark wooden bar and a burly, grim-faced barman.

'Gen'lemen?' he asked, in a rasping voice that sounded like a threat.

'We're looking for Daniel Hide.'

'Never heard of him,' said the barman. 'What are you drinking?'

'If he comes by, tell him Peter Willis and his brother were here looking for him.' He tapped Ben on the arm and they made to leave.

'Hold your horses,' said a voice from a room to their right.

Ben turned to see a man step out, ducking under the low doorway as he did so. The stranger took a deep breath, half closing his eyes, and then grabbed Peter by the throat.

'Just the two of you?' he asked quietly, looking at Ben. Peter choked and grimaced, turning beetroot.

'Aye', said Ben.

'You weren't followed?'

'No.'

'You're sure?'

'Aye', said Ben, looking at Peter, whose eyes were rolling back into his skull.

'Good', said the smuggler, letting go of Peter. He staggered back, holding his neck and gasping like a cat with a fur ball. The smuggler whistled and five men appeared from the shadows.

'Let's see what you have then', he said, putting a battered hat on his head and walking towards the door. Ben cast a worried glance at Peter, who, to his amazement, was smiling.

'Don't worry, brother', he said with a cough. 'I'm right here.'

They took the smugglers to the boat and Hide, their leader, carefully examined the merchandise, sampling the brandy and tobacco like a connoisseur. When he had satisfied himself of the quality and nodded his approval to his men, he turned to Ben and Peter.

'That's good stuff,' he said.

'Then we are in business?' said Peter.

'But here's the thing,' said the smuggler with a sigh. 'What's to stop my colleagues and I simply gutting you like a couple of herring and taking these here goods of yours?'

'Because,' said Peter coolly, 'there wouldn't be any more.'

'So?' said the smuggler. 'We got lots of suppliers.'

'Of gut-rot gin maybe,' said Peter. 'I can get you port wine. I can get you silk. I can get you opium.'

The smuggler grinned.

'I like you,' he said, nodding at Peter. 'But I don't like you,' he said, turning to Ben. 'Twins ain't natural and there's something about you . . .'

'Yeah, well,' said Peter. 'The deal's with both of us, so we'll all have to learn to get along.'

There was a tense silence for a few minutes until Hide nodded again and gestured for his men to unload the boat. This was done with military efficiency. Another boat was brought round and within minutes the smugglers were set to leave.

Hide took a leather purse from his pocket, weighed it and tossed it to Peter, who opened it and looked inside with his usual dimpled grin.

'There's more where that came from, friend,' said Hide.

'Until next time, then,' said Peter.

'Aye,' said Hide, stepping into the boat. 'Don't linger in these parts. The customs men are afoot and they are animals, believe me. One of their number was killed in the line of duty not two weeks ago. They are in a dark mood.'

He looked at Ben as the boat rowed away.

'If you get caught, don't mention that you ever saw us. If you do, I'll have you gelded.'

As soon as the smugglers were out of earshot, Ben began cursing his brother. He shoved him angrily, but Peter laughed him off, which made Ben all the more furious.

'Calm yourself,' chuckled Peter. 'They are all right.'

'They are cut-throats!' hissed Ben. 'They'll hang one day – and us alongside them if you're not careful.'

'What's all this talk of hanging?' said Peter. 'No one's going to hang. The brandy we gave 'em will end up in the cellars of the Justice of the Peace and the Member of Parliament and the Lord of the Manor. No one hangs smugglers round here, Benjy-boy.

They might flog the odd one for appearances' sake, but nothing more. You worry too much.'

'You heard what he said about the customs men,' said Ben.

'He was just trying to scare us,' said Peter with a dimpled grin. 'And it looks like he's succeeded. But don't worry, brother of mine. I'm here. I'm always here.' He held the purse in front of him and jingled the contents. 'And we've just made a year's wages, maybe two. It calls for a celebration.'

'You ain't thinking of going back to the Black Horse?'

'Lord, no,' said Peter. 'We'll go to the Fox and Hounds. It's only up the lane a little. Come on, cheer up.'

Peter started to walk away and, after a moment's hesitation, Ben followed him.

'I just don't like spending time with people like that,' said Ben sulkily.

'Like what?' said Peter, kicking a small pebble into the creek they were walking beside. 'You mean people like the ones who gave us all that money for the stuff we stole from the ship? No one made you come along, did they? No one made you take the money. You ain't much different.'

Ben stopped in his tracks.

'I think I am.'

'You *want* to be better than them, I know,' said Peter amiably. 'You think yourself better than them – better than me – but from where I'm standing you're still a rogue, ain't you?'

Peter grinned at his brother.

'The fact is you keep getting yourself into all kinds of mess, and I'm always there to help you. You've clearly forgotten that this venture was your idea in the first place.'

'My idea?' Ben shouted. 'It never was.' But he did have a vague recollection of talking to Tubbs, the quartermaster . . . No – it could not have been his notion. This was just another of Peter's tricks he always employed to shift the blame.

'Don't worry, Benjy-boy,' he said. 'Peter's here. I'm always here and always will be. That's what brothers are for.'

Ben looked away, scowling into the setting sun.

'But maybe we ought to turn over a new leaf, you and me?' said Peter mischievously. 'Maybe we ought to throw this money into the creek?'

Ben turned to face his brother, who was leaning out over a slimy mud bank, tossing the purse into the air. Peter smiled his wide smile, daring Ben to come and snatch it. However, one of the throws was somewhat misjudged and in his effort to catch the purse Peter went slithering down the bank and into the clinging slime of the marsh, instantly sinking to his waist.

Ben laughed as Peter cursed and yelled at him to help him out, enjoying the comic spectacle of his brother waist-deep in the grey ooze.

'Stop laughing and help me out,' shouted Peter as he flailed about, his coat sleeves flicking gobbets of mud as he did so.

'Hush,' said Ben. 'You'll have the locals on us.'

Ben did make a move in his direction, but it was hard not to slip himself, and seeing even in that dim light how swiftly Peter's legs had sunk beneath the slime, he grew suddenly fearful and backed away. There was something about that mud and the thought of being sucked down into it that filled him with horror.

It was then Ben noticed the purse which Peter had dropped as he had fallen: the precious purse with all the takings. And it had landed on the firm earth of the track. Peter followed the course of Ben's gaze and saw the workings of his mind as clear as if they were tattooed across his brother's face.

'Get me out of here,' he hissed, the mud already up to his chest, a note of panic appearing in his voice for the first time. He reached out towards the bank, trying in vain to find some purchase in the surrounding sludge. 'And you can have the lot. I swear – you can have all there is.'

But Peter said these words with little conviction and he saw the wry smile on Ben's face as he picked up the money and put it in his pocket. Peter had naught to bargain with, as he no longer held the purse or had the means to take it back.

'Get me out, you bastard! Now!' he spat. 'Or so help me . . .'

'Or so help you what?' said Ben, his voice not quite as bold as his words and his hands suddenly sweating. 'Strikes me you ain't in no position to bargain.'

'I'll kill you!' he snarled, his face already purple with rage. 'I'll kill you stone dead!'

'I don't think so,' said Ben, turning up the collar of his coat against the chill breeze that now blew across the marshes.

'So you'd see me die, would you?' said Peter, slapping his hands down on the surface of the mud and splashing his face. 'And you all high and mighty about them smugglers. Ain't this murder, then?'

'I ain't laid a finger on you,' said Ben coldly. 'I ain't touched you.'

Peter took a deep breath and grinned his dim-pled grin.

'Come on, Ben', he said. 'We're brothers, ain't we? More than brothers – we're twins. We're like two parts of the one thing, Ben. And you've got to admit: I've always been there when you needed me. I've always been there and I always will be.'

Ben seemed hardly to be listening. He was look-ing around for something, and then strode down the track and returned a few seconds later with a long pole.

'That's it, Ben', said Peter with relief. 'That's using the old thinking tackle.'

Ben eased the pole towards his brother, passing it through his hands inch by inch until it was just in front of Peter's grinning face, and then he jerked it forwards, hitting him sharply in the nose and stun-ning him.

Blood began to drip immediately from Peter's nose. Ben hit him again. With mud in his face and the blow from the pole, Peter could barely focus on his brother and was still trying to make sense of the vague shapes in front of him when the end of the pole was thrust into his chest and Ben began to push with all his strength, shoving Peter away from the bank and further into the mud.

Peter tried to wrest the pole from Ben's grip, but to no avail. His arms were heavy with the weight of the wet mud, his hands slippery. He was exhausted. Finished.

'Well then,' said Peter bitterly, spitting blood, the mud rising up his chin. 'If I'm to die here, I'll take you with me.'

'And how do you plan to do that?' said Ben, shoving the pole hard into his breastbone.

'You remember those customs men?' he hissed. 'They'll be looking to avenge their murdered comrade. How's it going to lie for you when they catch you with all that money out here in the marshes?'

Ben stared at him.

'You said the smugglers were only trying to scare us,' said Ben. 'And anyway – how would they find me?'

'Help!' Peter suddenly yelled. 'Smugglers! *Help!* '

Ben hit his brother's shouting face with the end of the pole and pressed down with all his might until the mud was sucked into Peter's gaping mouth and his cries turned to muddy gurgles. His wide eyes bulged brightly in his filthy face, twitching with fury and fear. One more shove and Peter would slide even deeper into the sludge, swallowed up by the marsh with a hungry slurp, until no

ripple or bubble remained to show he had ever been there.

But to Ben's horror lantern lights began to appear, bobbing about on the far horizon like fireflies. He was panic-struck. He had heard those smuggler-hunters sometimes had dogs with them and maybe they were even on horseback – and they would certainly know the marshes better than he would.

He threw down the pole and ran, cursing Peter all the while. He ran without daring to turn round and saw that he was heading back towards the Black Horse tavern. Then he noticed an upturned boat near the path and, lifting one side up, he dived underneath.

Ben lay there, listening to the sound of his own heart beating. He listened for Peter's shouting voice but there was only silence. And then, suddenly, he heard footsteps, and through the narrow gap between the side of the boat and the earth he saw booted feet. It was the customs men.

He heard their muttering, grumbling voices as they walked past, but there was no mention of Peter, only of a wasted hunt, of tired legs and a thirst for the ale they were intending to drink.

They must have walked past the creek where

Peter had fallen in. They could hardly have missed him, despite the failing light. Ben was forced to come to the conclusion that Peter had slipped beneath the surface of the mud, and he felt a feeling of glorious release, as if a great weight had been taken from his back.

Satisfied that the customs men had moved on, Ben scrabbled out from beneath the boat. He would need to row back to the ship before night fell so blackly that he would lose all sense of direction. He ran full tilt, running to escape the oncoming night, not giving the merest glance to the creek where his brother lay consumed by mud.

When Ben got back to the ship, the quartermaster pulled him aside.

'Where the hell have you been?' he said, grabbing Ben by the throat, checking to see that no one else was around. A nearby lantern gave the scene an eerie glow in the surrounding darkness. 'The captain'll be back soon. Where's my money?'

'I haven't got your money! The smugglers double-crossed us. It was all I could do to get out of there with my life. Look at me,' he said, pointing to the mud stains that covered his clothes.

Tubbs used his free hand to search Ben's pockets

and it did not take him long to find the purse. He let Ben go and tipped the purse into his open palm. But instead of coins, grey mud poured from it. The quartermaster shook the sludge from his hand and grabbed Ben again, who stared at the purse in bafflement.

'What's this?' snarled Tubbs. 'Are you out to cheat me, boy? And where's that brother of yours?'

'Customs men got him,' said Ben, recovering his wits. 'That's what I'm trying to tell you. I only just got away myself. Peter wasn't so lucky.'

'And how am I going to explain that to the captain?' he said.

Ben had already given this a little thought.

'Just say he got homesick,' he said. 'Say he means to stay with his old friends and give up the seafaring life.'

The quartermaster froze, thinking for a moment or two. There was something about Ben that made him nervous. He didn't trust him or his brother.

'I don't know what's going on,' said Tubbs, prodding Ben in the chest, 'but no one makes a fool out of me. You and your brother owe me, and one way or another you'd better pay up or so help me you'll wish the customs men *had* got you as well.'

The quartermaster stomped away, leaving Ben

staring at the empty purse he had tossed to the floor. He did not understand. Peter must have tricked him – but how? He had heard it jangle. The captain, having just returned to the ship a little worse for drink, suddenly grabbed him by the arm.

'Look at you, you filthy oaf,' he said. 'Which one of you is it anyway?'

'Peter, sir,' said Ben. 'I mean, Ben, sir.'

'Are you trying to be clever, boy?' said the captain.

'No, sir,' said Ben.

Ben went below. Peter's hammock was empty. Ben climbed into his, taking a knife with him just in case. He tried to stay awake but exhaustion got the better of him and he fell asleep, waking what seemed like minutes later (but was in fact hours), panicked and confused.

There was something wrong with his hammock. At first he thought that he was lying in his own blood, but he soon realised that it was not blood at all. His hammock was filled with mud – wet, stinking marsh mud.

Ben climbed out of the hammock and went up on deck as dawn broke over the cold North Sea, staggering out into the half-light, nauseous and dazed. Bemused faces stared back at him. The captain strode over, looking him up and down as if he could not quite believe his eyes as mud dripped from Ben's clothes.

'Get that mud cleaned off and swab the deck,' he said. 'And do a good job or I'll throw you *and* your brother overboard.'

'Did the quartermaster not tell you, then, sir?' said Ben.

The captain had already started to walk away and now turned back to face him.

'Ah, yes,' he said. 'Your little nonsense about your brother running off home. He did mention it, yes.'

'But, sir,' said Ben, 'I swear –'

'You'd swear just about anything with the right encouragement, I dare say,' said the captain, spitting on the deck at Ben's feet. 'But whatever joke you're having with Tubbs, don't play the same trick on me, for I saw your brother with my own eyes not five minutes ago.'

With that, the captain turned on his heels and strode off, leaving Ben staring after him, a cold hand grabbing his heart and squeezing tight. Peter had escaped somehow. He had escaped the marsh and the customs men – though God alone knew how – and had returned to the ship with revenge in his blood. It must have been him that put the mud in Ben's hammock. One thing was for certain: he could not sit and wait for the marlinspike that would no doubt be harpooning his gullet that day or the next.

Ben searched the ship for his brother, his mind buzzing like a beehive. How had Peter dragged himself out of the creek? He must have found a boat and stolen it and made his way back to the ship. And now Peter was going to kill him as soon as he got the chance, Ben was sure of it.

But however hard he searched he saw no sign of his brother. Perhaps the captain – who everyone knew was fond of a drink – was mistaken. He hoped so. Ben swabbed the deck as he was told, looking about him for any sign of Peter as the ship set sail for Holland.

There was no sign of Peter on deck, below or above it. Then Ben noticed that there were footprints striding right across the deck he had just worked hard to clean.

How could it be? How, when they were now miles from the coast, could someone leave a trail of mud like this?

'I thought I told you to get this clean,' said the captain, walking past.

'Aye aye, sir,' said Ben. Peter was trying to scare him. He was on the ship; Ben could sense him.

Somehow he had got himself out of that bog and back on board.

Ben spent the rest of the morning looking over his shoulder, twitching and starting at every splash and rope creak. At last he glimpsed the familiar figure of his brother walking towards the stern of the ship. He ran to confront him, tripping over a pail of water and barging past two of his crewmates, who cursed him as he stood looking at empty space, his brother having seemingly vanished into thin air.

This was repeated throughout the rest of the day. Ben caught a flash of Peter climbing down into the hold, but when he got there the hold was empty. He saw him standing among a group of sailors, but when the men parted to return to work, Peter was gone.

'Come on,' said the captain, slapping him on the arm and making him jump. 'Do some work! Get up and have a look at the main topsail. Shadbolt thought he saw a tear.'

Ben set about climbing the rigging.

He reached the main topsail yard: the great horizontal beam across the mainmast from which hung the topsail. He always loved being high among the sails and, now, even the fear of Peter started to dissipate. He felt like a bird up there, the white sails puffed out and billowing like clouds all around him. Then he turned to see a familiar figure standing along the yard.

'Peter . . . I just meant to teach you a lesson,' said Ben, his speech prepared. 'I was never going to really . . .' His voice tailed off as he looked at his brother.

Peter was smiling at him. He was still covered from head to foot in foul-smelling mud, which trickled in slow gobbets down his face and dripped from his sodden clothes. Ben watched, horror-struck, as mud dribbled into his brother's eyes and he did not blink.

'For God's sake, Peter,' said Ben. 'You look . . .'

'Don't worry,' gurgled Peter. 'I'm here, brother. I'll always be here.' His mouth widened into a dimpled grin and mud oozed horribly between his teeth and down over his chin. He opened his mouth further and the mud flooded out, pouring down his chest in an unending, glutinous stream.

Ben let go of the ropes to shield his face as Peter lurched towards him, and he fell backwards through the air, the scream dying in his throat as his head struck the deck with a sickening crack that stopped the whole ship's crew like a musket firing.

A fall from the rigging was not unheard of, but unusual on such a calm and gentle day. And though the broken face was hard to bear, many mariners had seen worse in their time. No, what drew puzzled and nervous glances from the onlookers was the fact that they were certain they had seen only one sailor fall, and yet here were the twins lying dead, lying on their sides, their knees bent to their chests as if still in the womb. Stranger still, a great swathe of foul-smelling mud covered the bodies, mingling with the crimson blood that seeped across the deck.

'What a horrible way to die', said Cathy when Thackeray had finished.

'Which?' he said with a grin. 'In a muddy creek or falling from a ship's mast?'

'Either', said Cathy. 'Have you ever killed a man, Thackeray?'

'Cathy!' I hissed. 'What sort of question is that to ask a person?'

But I was not concerned for the impropriety of the question, but by the dread of what answer might be forthcoming. To my horror, though not my surprise, Thackeray nodded slowly.

'I have killed,' he said. 'But I take no pride in it. I was on a Navy ship and those I killed, I killed in battle. And war makes murderers of us all.'

Cathy stared, wide-eyed.

'Did you shoot them, sir?' she said. 'Or run them through with your sword?'

'You're a bloodthirsty maid, aren't you?' he answered with a chuckle. 'That's too much story-reading for you. It puts dark thoughts in your head.'

'But it's just so exciting.'

'It may seem so,' he said a little sadly.

I listened to this conversation with mounting anxiety. I had been given strict instructions to let no one in, and now I discovered I had let a self-confessed killer – Navy man or not – into our house. Even when our father did return, what guarantee was there that he would be equal to the task of dealing with Thackeray?

'You say "*was* on a Navy ship", Mr Thackeray,' I said. 'Do you serve no longer? And why then do you still wear the uniform?'

'I sail aboard a different ship now, Ethan,' he answered. 'I serve a different captain.'

'You are a deserter, then?' I said coldly. 'Is that why you are so mysterious?'

'No, Ethan,' said Thackeray. 'I'm no deserter. And I will thank you not to accuse me twice.'

'I thought you said it wasn't polite to pry into Mr Thackeray's business, Ethan,' said Cathy.

'No harm done, miss,' he said with what would have passed for a warm smile in a less frigid countenance. 'I'm a stranger in your house. Ethan has every right to be suspicious.'

'Yet still you do not answer, I notice,' I said. 'Why is it then that you wear the uniform of the Royal Navy?'

Thackeray took a deep breath and sighed loudly as if running out of patience with a bothersome infant.

'I was little more than a boy when I enlisted as a midshipman,' he said. 'And little more than a boy when I went into battle.'

'It must have been horrible,' said Cathy. 'Were you very frightened?'

'I'm not ashamed to say I was, Miss Cathy,' he replied. 'There are no fearless men in a battle. Only a liar would say different. I have seen seasoned men – fighting men – vomit with fear as the enemy sailed into range and the cannons boomed. I have seen men – good men – reduced to bloody meat.'

Once again Thackeray seemed lost in his memories. Or at least he affected the air of a man lost in memories. I was deeply mistrustful of all he said and did and I noted that none of his words went in any way to explain why it was he still wore a Navy uniform, or indeed what manner of sailor he now was.

'Ah, look,' said Cathy, clumsily endeavouring to change the subject. 'The wind seems to be dying.'

'Aye,' said Thackeray, glancing at the window and then at me. 'I do believe the storm is dropping off a little. Perhaps I may take my leave of you, then.'

'No,' said Cathy to my utter consternation. 'It is still raining and it is still frightful. We wouldn't hear of it, would we, Ethan?'

Thackeray smiled at me in a most disturbing way.

'No,' I said. 'Of course not.'

'And since you're staying, Thackeray,' said Cathy, 'you can tell us another story.'

'And what would you like a story about, Miss Cathy?' he said.

'Pirates!' she answered without hesitation. 'Have you ever met a pirate on your travels?'

'Hush now, Cathy,' I said, blushing at her

foolishness. 'How could he? The days of pirates are long gone.'

'Well now', said Thackeray with an annoyingly patronising tone. 'There'll always be pirates, Ethan, as long as there are ships on the sea.'

'I suppose you are right', I said. 'But I meant the *real* age of pirates, sir – the age of Rackham, Kidd and Blackbeard.'

Thackeray smiled and his gold tooth winked.

'You're familiar with your pirates, then?'

'Oh yes', said Cathy. 'A *General History of the Robberies and Murders of the Most Notorious Pirates* is a special favourite of ours.'

'You know the book, sir?' I asked.

'Captain Johnson's book? Aye, I know it. A right scholarly account it is too, they say. But it is incomplete.'

'Incomplete?' I said.

'Well, it must be, must it not?' he said. 'For there is no mention, I think I am correct in saying, of Captain Reeve.'

Cathy and I exchanged a puzzled glance.

'Who is Captain Reeve?' asked Cathy. 'Was he a pirate?'

'Only the most fearsome pirate that ever sailed Neptune's oceans', said Thackeray. 'As a matter of fact I have a tale that concerns that very person. Would you like to hear it?'

'I am sure we would,' said Cathy, and I nodded my agreement.

'Very well, then,' he said. 'I'll begin . . .'

THE
MONKEY

One fine June day the Fox, a small brig out of
Boston, Massachusetts, was intercepted on its way
to Hispaniola by a vessel flying a red flag featuring
a skull and a black heart.

The pirates boarded the Fox and herded the crew
together on the weather deck. For what seemed
like hours they were made to stand in the sun, their
guards grinning at their discomfort as they lolled in
the shade of the foresail and made a great show of
studying their pistols and cutlasses.

Among the Fox's crew was a boy of about thirteen
– he was never sure of his birth date; a boy called

Lewis Jackson. He was watching the ransacking of the ship with great interest.

A sudden hush came upon the ship, and the grinning guards lost their easy ways and stood to attention – or at least some rough, loose-limbed pirate version of attention. Slowly, out of the deepest part of the shadows, walked the man who was their leader.

Lewis saw that he was a tall man, easily the tallest aboard that ship from either crew; he was tall and lean in his tallness, long-limbed with a hungry but easy cat-like gait.

His eyes were heavy-lidded and deep-set, but their pale blueness shone out from the shadows. He wore no hat, but had a red scarf tied about his head. Gold earrings hung from his earlobes and gold armlets glistened on his wrists and biceps.

'Now then, lads', he said with a grin. 'I'll talk straight and not veer from that course. We're all mariners here. Your ship has been taxed by Tobias Reeve. Some of you might know me as Blackheart Reeve.'

A murmur ran through the crew. Everyone had indeed heard that name; all who worked the seas from Maine to Panama were taught to fear its mention.

'Blackheart', he continued, clearly well rehearsed in this speech, 'on account of the death's head and black heart flag we flies . . '. Here he paused for effect and his grin widened. 'And likewise on account of my reported cruel nature.'

Lewis remembered the tales he had heard in bars and taverns, stories of piracy and of the merciless killing ways of Blackheart Reeve himself. The word was he had already killed a hundred men and showed no signs of stopping.

'Now I said I'd steer a straight course and a true one, and I won't tell you I ain't killed more than my fair share, but I ain't never hanged a man like those Navy cowards do, nor flogged a man to death neither. Every man I killed looked into my eyes before he met his maker, and that's the God's honest truth.'

Lewis could see that the crew did not take these words as any special comfort, but he found himself in secret admiration of this pirate.

'I'm sure you are all brave men and might feel it your duty to resist us as we relieve your vessel of any valuables as might be aboard. We are fighting men ourselves and we understand that and we respect it – don't we, boys?'

The pirate crew murmured in assent.

'But it is *my* duty to tell you that any resistance

will be fatal to those who do the resisting.' Blackheart smiled a wide and generous smile. 'Think of your wives and sweethearts and leave us to go about our business. You have my word that none will be harmed who do not stand in our way.'

So it was that the pirates went about their work, stripping the Fox of anything they thought of value. When they had taken everything they wanted, Blackheart clapped his hands together with a loud crack.

'Now then, my good fellows,' he said. 'We must bid you a fond adieu. It is a tradition with us that we ask the crew of any ship we take if there be any among their number who would sail with us. Well, boys? Is there any of you who wants to be a free man?'

'I think I speak for my crew,' said the captain of the Fox, 'when I say that none here would sail with you, even if their very lives depended on it.'

'Is that so?' said Blackheart. 'Is that true, lads? Ain't there a man among you who wants to live the buccaneer life, where each man gets his honest share of all we take and each man gets a fair say in how we go about our business?'

'I have given you our answer –' began the captain until a cocked pistol interrupted him.

'I'm asking these men, not you,' said Blackheart.

'I'll sail with you, sir,' said a man to Lewis's left, a man from Newfoundland called Green.

'Welcome, brother,' said Blackheart. 'And you need never say "sir" again. "Captain" is good enough for me or any man.'

'I'll see you hanged for this, Green,' said the *Fox*'s captain. 'This is mutiny. This is –'

'Shut your mouth or it'll be you that's hanging from your own bowsprit,' Blackheart snarled.

'I thought you did not hang people,' said the captain.

'Nor do I, friend.' Blackheart grinned. 'It will be your own men that do the deed. Now quiet – before I lose my patience with you. Anyone else who wants to live the free life?'

'Aye,' came another voice – a voice it took Lewis a moment to realise was his own.

'Lewis,' hissed the captain. 'What are you doing?'

The pirates laughed as Lewis stepped forward, but Blackheart waved his pistol and bade them leave off.

'Now then, boys,' said Blackheart. 'I reckon that if this lad has the balls to speak out, we should have the balls to take him on. Welcome to the good life, Lewis.'

Blackheart turned back to the crew of the *Fox*.

'There ain't much in the way of vittles, but we've left you enough water to last you until you get back to shore.'

'I suppose we should be grateful, then?' said the *Fox*'s captain.

Blackheart's grin disappeared in an instant.

'You should be grateful I don't blow your ear off, for I don't take kindly to being talked to in that fashion. You shall apologise.'

'I don't think I shall,' said the captain.

'You're a brave man, I'll give you that,' said Blackheart. 'Ain't he brave, boys?'

The pirates murmured their assent as always. Then Blackheart raised his pistol and pulled the trigger, and the captain dropped to the floor like a rag doll. Lewis stared at the fallen body and then followed the pirates to the boat that would take them to his new ship, the *Firefly*.

'That bother you, boy?' said Blackheart later as the pirates sailed away. 'The shooting of your captain back there?'

'No,' said Lewis. And though it was bravado when he had formed the words, it was the simple truth by the time they left his lips. He had not been bothered at all. Excited, perhaps – thrilled even – but not bothered. 'He was a mean man, quick to flog. Good riddance to him.'

Blackheart grinned and slapped him on the back. 'You'll do,' he said. 'You'll do.'

And so began Lewis Jackson's career as a pirate. No apprenticeship was served, for only minutes after he and Green were elected to become part of their crew, the *Firefly* was speeding towards another ship.

It was a ship bringing families from old England to a better life in New England. Lewis could feel fear and hatred emanating from the passengers and crew like heat, and it felt strange: not pleasant, but not wholly unpleasant either.

A minister in a powdered wig waved his Bible at them and called them minions of Satan until Blackheart slapped him across the bridge of his nose with a pistol butt.

'You are spawn of the Devil!' the minister shouted at them as they left with their booty. 'You'll see the torments of hell!'

Lewis laughed as heartily as any of the pirate crew as the minister's voice faded away into the distance. They had had a good haul and no trouble from the crew or their saintly cargo. But Lewis was about to learn that not all ships give up their treasures quite so willingly.

Two days after they fleeced the colonists, they came across a merchant ship heading for the Chesapeake Bay. Blackheart ordered them to give chase, and they closed in on their prize with ease. But the captain and crew of this ship had been boarded before and they were not about to let it happen again. They had cannons and they knew how to use them.

The first blast struck the *Firefly* amidships, holing her at the waterline. The pirates stood agog, shocked to a man that their prey should bite back with such unexpected ferocity.

The second shot struck the gunwales near the stern and knocked Lewis sideways. His ears roared with the noise and he pulled a four inch long splinter from his thigh. Green, the Newfoundlander who'd joined the pirates with him from the *Fox*, was not so lucky. Lewis saw his body lying in a pool of blood. He saw his head in another on the far side of the deck.

The *Firefly* was mortally wounded, but luckily the ship they had sought to take was happy to escape to the safety of Chesapeake Bay. The crew cheered and jeered as they sailed away, leaving the *Firefly* to limp along, licking its wounds.

Blackheart knew full well that once news reached the authorities that his ship was crippled they would send the Navy to take him. They would all be hanging from a gibbet in Charleston if they did not put clear water between themselves and the shore.

'We need a new ship, boys', said Blackheart. 'And we needs her fast.'

The *Firefly* headed south and was off the Carolinas when they spied a ship on the horizon. It was Lewis himself who had spotted it from his perch high up in the crow's nest.

Blackheart emerged from his cabin with the hungry look of a wolf. He had a telescope under one arm and, after seeing where the ship lay, he put it to his eye.

'Look lively, then, boys', he said as Lewis climbed down on to the deck, trying to ready himself for whatever fight lay in store.

Blackheart ordered a warning shot to be fired across its bow. He was taking no chances now. They had to be prepared this time. But all the same, he could not risk damaging what would be their new vessel if all went well.

But the ship paid no heed. It made no move to surrender or escape. The sails were furled as if it were in port instead of out on the high seas. Lewis could see no sign of movement aboard the vessel at all and it was not long before the men about him began to mutter suspiciously.

For all the tough and fearless ways of the pirate life, a buccaneer can be as superstitious as any other mariner, and it was hard not to be wary of this strange desolate ship.

Blackheart was of a more rational disposition, however, and he began to suspect that this might be the bait in some unseen trap. He had men climb the masts and search the horizons, but there was not another ship in sight. The fleetest ship in all the Navy could not have caught the *Firefly* from such a distance.

Blackheart then turned to consider the notion that the crew of the mysterious ship had seen their approach and, guessing their intention, had hidden themselves out of sight, ready to attack them once they began to board. Even now, there might be hidden cannons ready to be blasted.

It was a dilemma to be sure. The *Firefly* was struggling. Water was filling the holds and she was beginning to list perilously. Blackheart had no choice. This ship was their only chance.

He ordered a boarding party to man the small

sailing boat they sometimes used to lead an attack and he himself would take her across. Lewis watched them arm themselves to the teeth with swords and axes and pistols, and he could see by their faces that they were preparing themselves for death or killing. Then Blackheart told Lewis that he was to be one of the boarding party.

'Me?' said Lewis. 'But –'

'Come on!' said Blackheart, thumping him in the chest. 'Your first boarding! Best day of your life. I can remember mine like it was yesterday!'

There was nothing more to be said. Lewis knew he had no choice. He picked out a hatchet that he felt looked especially menacing and climbed aboard the boat with the others.

During the whole of the short journey across to the ship, Lewis was flinching as if a shot or cannon blast was forever about to strike the boat, and he avowed that if he was ever part of another boarding, he would pay more attention to the seating arrangements and not be foolish enough to sit in the prow.

If sailing across was fraught with apprehension, then climbing aboard the ship was doubly so. Blackheart was fearless and bounded aboard as if he already owned the ship and had every right to stand on her decks. He halloed in his loudest voice, but there was no reply. He halloed again. Nothing.

Lewis could see that this was no usual boarding. The pirates were as wary as he was, clearly fearing an ambush. Blackheart sent a small party down into the holds to search for crew members, telling them in a loud voice to cut the throat of the first person they found unless the rest of the crew made themselves known that instant. But nothing stirred and the pirates found no one on their search. The ship was deserted.

The pirates regrouped on the weather deck, each man wearing the same puzzled and apprehensive expression.

'What's goin' on, Cap'n?' said a man called Murnau.

'I don't rightly know,' said Blackheart.

Suddenly there was a great rending sound and the *Firefly* keeled over and began to sink with shocking speed. They heard the cries of their crewmates as she went down and those who fell clear were dragged under by the sinking vessel.

'Damn it!' shouted Blackheart. 'But I loved that ship!'

Lewis could only think about the drowned men

and how close to going down with her he had been. Like most of the men aboard the *Firefly*, he had never learned to swim.

Blackheart rallied his men. A seaworthy ship was treasure enough on this occasion, but that did not stop the pirates from searching for more and once again they moved about the strange deserted ship.

Lewis followed Blackheart down into the hold, dark enough and seeming all the more Stygian after the daylight's bright blazing above. They both squinted into the gloom, but it was the smell that Lewis noted first: a smell he could not place but that for some reason made his skin crawl.

On closer inspection they could see that the hold was full of boxes, crates and jars containing nuts and seeds, shells, rocks and even earth. Blackheart looked at Lewis and raised an eyebrow.

'What the hell is all this?' he said. 'And were they taking it somewhere or bringing it back?'

Lewis and Blackheart spotted the cage at the same time. It was a sturdy if crudely made construction, a cube of about three feet square with stout sticks for bars bound together by some kind of tough vine. But the vine had snapped and the door swung open.

'What was in that, I wonder?' said Blackheart grimly.

Just at that moment there was a movement at the other end of the hold and Blackheart pulled a pistol from his waistband and cocked it – then another movement, like a large mouse scurrying. Something careered out of the hold at rare speed, its feet pattering like a drum roll on the steps.

'What the devil is it?' said Blackheart, sounding nervous for the first time since Lewis had met him. Suddenly there was a shout from above.

'Captain! Come quick.'

Blackheart, his pistol still raised, began to scale the steps out of the hold two at a time. Lewis practically threw himself on to the deck after him, where he came face to face with the reason for all the shouting.

Lying on his back in the baking sun was a pirate called Gower, though Lewis only knew it to be him because of the gaudy clothes he perpetually wore and the garland of necklaces draped across his chest. For Gower's face and body were bloated like he had been dead for days instead of minutes, and blue-black as if a mighty beating had been the cause.

'What happened?' said Blackheart as Lewis

scrabbled to his feet.

'There was a damned monkey,' said one of the men. 'It bit him. Couple of minutes later he cries out and I find him like this.'

The crew scowled at the black and bloated body.

'At least we know what was in that cage now,' said Blackheart.

Suddenly Gower's eyes flicked open and the crew flinched.

'Help . . . me,' said Gower, his eyes wild with terror.

'He's alive!' gasped Lewis.

Blackheart turned to the crew. 'I want that monkey dead – understand?'

'Aye, Captain!' said the pirates and they set off in search of the creature, pistols cocked and cutlasses drawn.

Gower was trying to say something, but he could not get the words out and a white froth bubbled at his lips. Blackheart and Lewis crouched at his side and strained their ears to hear.

'Kill . . . me,' he finally said, and looked at them with tear-filled eyes.

Blackheart nodded, pulled out a long knife and plunged it with fearful suddenness and strength into his crewmate's chest, pressing down until all signs of life disappeared from Gower's face.

'I sailed with him for twenty years or more,' said Blackheart, without looking round at Lewis. 'I'm going to kill that animal myself, gut it, skin it and cut it into tiny pieces.'

A pistol shot rang out towards the stern and Lewis and Blackheart ran to its sound. The pirates were pointing up at the top of the mizzenmast. There was the monkey, staring down, teeth bared.

But understandably no man was keen to go up the rigging after him, and three more shots proved him to be a difficult target.

'Put a bowl of water on the deck there. He'll come down when he's thirsty,' said Blackheart. 'Then we'll have him.'

Blackheart posted two men with cocked pistols to watch at a safe distance and then went with Lewis and a couple of other men to search the officers' cabins.

The cabins were in a state of disarray. One of the crew speculated that perhaps other pirates had attacked the ship before them and taken the crew or killed them and thrown them overboard.

But the cabins did not look as though they had been searched for valuables. The disturbance was too arbitrary and violent. Besides, there were valuables lying about on the floor for all to see. Then Lewis happened upon a book that fell open as he searched, many of its pages ripped or torn and those remaining soaked in some sort of sticky liquid. He started to examine it.

Blackheart walked by and asked Lewis what he was reading. Lewis told him that it was the journal of a gentleman explorer whom the ship had taken aboard at some island in the Indies.

The journal detailed the many seeds and so on he had collected on his travels – the evidence of which was in the hold – but the writer had devoted most of his energy to describing the '*marvellous specimen*', the '*most extraordinary creature*' he had captured on the island. On a torn fragment of one of the pages, Lewis read how he was going to take it back to England and exhibit it at the Royal Society. His writing became giddy with excitement as he talked about the looks on the faces of his rivals.

'Damn and blast him!' said Blackheart. 'What the hell would anyone want to bring a poisonous monkey back to England for?'

Lewis carried on reading. Another fragment spoke a little of how they had captured it, despite all the warnings from the natives, and had caged it and brought it aboard the ship.

Lewis turned the page. The journal came to an abrupt end. In a hasty and almost illegible scrawl were the words, 'God save us. It has escaped. I must'. And there it ended.

It was dusk now and light was fading fast. The sea was like molten copper, glowing with the fire from the setting sun. Lewis and the others walked back to the stern to see if the men had had any luck with the monkey, but instead they found one of them in a similar state to Gower, bruised all over and bloated. The other man was missing and though Blackheart's yell would have brought Satan himself running, he did not answer.

Blackheart thrust his cutlass into the bloated man's chest to finish him off.

'Throw him overboard,' he said, turning to a man called Vetch. 'Do the same with Gower. And keep an eye out for that monkey.'

'Aye, Captain,' said Vetch.

Vetch and another pirate hauled the corpse to the gunwales and threw him over, the body hitting the water with a loud splash. Then they went to get Gower's body, but returned moments later.

'He's gone,' said Vetch, his troubled face ghostly pale in the twilight.

'Who has?' said Blackheart.

'Gower,' said Vetch.

Blackheart cast a glance at Lewis and then back at Vetch, grabbing the man by his shirt.

'What nonsense is this?' said Blackheart, his voice wavering for the first time. 'How could he be gone?'

Vetch shrugged Blackheart's hand away.

'Well, he is!'

Blackheart put his hand to his forehead and stared at the deck as if hoping to find the answer scratched into the planks. Light seemed to be draining away by the second and Lewis could barely see beyond the nearest mast.

'Did any of you filthy swabs throw Gower overboard without my say-so?'

The crew were quick to deny doing any such thing, but this only caused more confusion and alarm among the pirates. Night was almost upon them, and each man felt a chill in the pit of his guts. Danger was second nature to men like these and they thrived on it, welcomed it. But this was different.

Lewis looked into the shadows beyond the reach of the lanterns that were now being lit against the onrush of night. He shivered at the thought that the monkey was out there somewhere, hidden from view but waiting to strike.

The idea of sleeping while that murderous beast was still loose seemed preposterous, but Blackheart knew that it was better to rest and keep their wits about them. He posted a watch of two men to stand guard at either side of the main group, who would do their best to sleep.

Lewis had thought the idea of sleep unimaginable, but had not realised how exhausted he was. Eventually the day took its toll and, though he tried hard to stay awake, after half an hour of watching the shadows for any trace of movement, his eyelids seemed to gain the weight of lead and he could not hold them open. His head lolled. His shallow fearful breathing turned to snores.

Lewis slept and dreamed. As if his brain welcomed the chance to escape the nightmare that had overtaken his waking life, he dreamed a happy sailor's dream of billowing sails against a blue sky. He dreamed of his own bravery in the capture of a ship. He led the attack, leaping over open sea, and shot the captain dead with his pistol before taking on the best part of the whole crew with a cutlass and forcing them to surrender. The holds were filled with gold and pearls and precious stones of every kind.

These happy adventures were brought to an abrupt end by the feel of soft fur against his cheek and he woke immediately, eyes blazing, knife in his hand. Did something scamper away? Or did he dream it all? Lewis wiped the cold sweat from his forehead and looked about him, disorientated. His shipmates were stirring, lit by the welcome glow of daybreak.

Slowly Lewis gathered his wits and joined the rest of the men as they stamped their feet and hugged themselves against the morning chill. The men who had stood watch joked about their hours on guard, but Lewis saw the ghost of the fear that still haunted their tense and ashen faces. Then he noticed something else. Only six men now stood on the weather deck. Blackheart had clearly noticed the same thing.

'Where's Murnau? And McCloud?' he shouted, his voice booming in the still air.

No one knew.

'This ship's cursed!' said Vetch, who was standing beside Lewis. There were murmurs of agreement.

'Well, you're free to swim for it,' said Blackheart, turning on him. 'Me, I'm for killing that –'

Blackheart suddenly broke off and looked at Lewis with an expression that was a frightening mix of fear, anger and madness. He drew a brace of pistols from his waistband and pointed them straight at his head.

'Captain?' said Lewis, taking a step backwards, but Blackheart pulled the triggers and there was a mighty blast and Lewis felt the whistling passage of the balls as they hurtled past his ears and the thump of something falling behind him. He turned to find the monkey lying on its back, one hole in its forehead, the other in its chest.

Despite his promise to anatomise the creature, Blackheart, wary of whatever poison filled the monkey's body, lifted it up on the end of a boat hook and unceremoniously tossed it overboard.

A great cheer went up among the pirates and after a moment's pause to recover from the shock of believing himself about to be shot, Lewis joined them.

Blackheart called for a celebration and grog was duly fetched and consumed with the usual piratical enthusiasm. There being a considerable amount of rum aboard, the surviving crew were soon in a state of profound intoxication.

The morning drifted lazily by. It was hot. The sun was directly overhead and branded any flesh that did not seek shadow. Lewis lay back against a mass of coiled rope and laughed at a joke he did not fully understand.

He realised that he had never felt so alive. He imagined that he could feel the very blood moving in his veins. To face death and cheat it: that was real life, lived to the full, and he pitied the dull land-lubbers in their shops and markets. He pitied their poor untested lives.

The danger aboard ship was over and Blackheart had to concern himself with the more mundane threat of being caught by the Navy and hanged, so after a goodly amount of time he roused his crew and told them it was time to set sail.

They were a small crew to be sure, but it was a small ship and they were skilled seamen. Lewis climbed the mainmast, looking down once or twice to see Hart and Prentice at the capstan, hauling the anchor, and the reassuring figure of Blackheart standing at the centre of the deck, hands on hips, barking commands.

Lewis continued his climb, pulling himself up on to the main yard so that he could unfurl the sail. As he did so his hands rested on something sticky, and he paused, wondering what it might be, when there was a cry so high and sharp it sounded like a woman's – though it must have been Hart or Prentice, because Lewis saw Blackheart draw his cutlass and run in that direction. Another scream rang out and then a pistol shot and then an awful silence.

'Captain!' he yelled, tugging at the rope to free the sail. 'Captain Blackheart, sir!'

And just at that moment, the knot came free and the sail came loose and fell down, revealing that inside it, like the tobacco in a cigar, was half a dozen bodies and the decomposing pieces of more, swaddled in silken threads. He recognised the startled face of Murnau before turning away with a cry of horror and looking down at the deck.

What he saw almost stopped his heart, and he knew there and then what had been in the crate. The spider scampered across the deck. Its body alone was as big as a large dog, and its great, long, many-jointed and bristled legs added horrifically to its size and nightmarish appearance. It stopped to look up at him with its eight black eyes and drummed its two front legs on the deck as a horse might paw the earth. As if in response, the first of the eggs, which Lewis could now see tucked among the remains of the crew, split open.

Cathy let out an involuntary whimper at the end of Thackeray's tale and it was only a supreme effort of will on my behalf that prevented a similar utterance emerging from my lips.

'Cathy has a particular horror of spiders,' I said.

Thackeray nodded, not with concern, as one might have expected, but with an expression that spoke more of satisfaction. It was as if he thought I had given him praise.

'Do such creatures exist?' said Cathy tremulously.

'Of course not, Cath,' I said, giving her a cuddle and looking to Thackeray for confirmation. But he simply snorted and took another drink.

'I thought you had a stronger stomach, miss,' said Thackeray. 'Perhaps you are both a mite young for these stories, after all.'

'Come now, sir,' I said. 'You are not so very much older than I am, I fancy.'

He leaned forward in the most intimidating manner.

'How old do you think I am?'

I ventured that I thought him to be in the order of seventeen or eighteen and to my surprise he roared with laughter, slapping the table and making his drink and my sister jump three inches in the air.

I could not for the life of me see what was so amusing about my reply and was about to say so in the strongest terms I felt able to, when he looked at us both in turn and I could see tears in his eyes.

'Tis a curious thing,' said Thackeray, 'but as dangerous a beast as the sea surely is, it has a magnetic pull on certain souls and to such as those there is no resisting its power.'

'Are you such a soul?' said Cathy.

'Aye,' said Thackeray. 'I yearned for brine as soon as I'd let go of my mother's tit – begging your pardon, Miss Cathy.'

Cathy blushed – not at the coarseness of Mr Thackeray's expression, but at his apology. No one had seen her worthy of an apology before.

'But not everyone can take the sea-road with ease,' said Thackeray. 'Some men are born to it, like I was – my father being a mariner and his father too – but others are not. Some men are trapped ashore, a sailor in a landlubber's body. There are few things sadder.'

Here he seemed to give me a special conspiratorial look that I resented, for how could this man know anything of my life? If I had forsaken a life at sea, I had done so willingly and he should mind his own business, for he knew nothing of mine. I was about to tell him so when Cathy spoke up.

'You said you were sweet on a girl,' she said. 'Would you have given up the sailor's life for her?'

'In a heartbeat, Miss Cathy,' he answered. 'In a heartbeat. But it was not to be. My father stood between us and would never have seen us wed. He said she was not good enough for me – but she was the loveliest girl a man could ever wish for. My father was a rich man, an important man. He persuaded her father to forbid her seeing me. She would not go against him.

'So she was betrothed to a man unworthy of her, a weak man. Still, I always believed she loved me best. though that is scant comfort. She had children with this creature. Children she might have had with me. Children who I would have loved and cherished.'

He broke off here and gave us such a piteous look.

'I went to sea to forget her, but the sea is no place to forget. A man has so much time to remember. I never saw her again – and never will now, rest her soul. When news reached me of her death, I was already ... already aboard my present ship.'

'And what became of the husband and the children?' asked Cathy.

'He took his own life,' said Thackeray bitterly. 'He was a weak man, as I said.'

'And the children?' said Cathy.

'This is a sad tale, miss,' said Thackeray. 'Let's dwell on it no further.'

'What was her name?' asked Cathy. 'Your sweetheart?'

'Mr Thackeray doesn't want to talk about it any more,' I said sharply, for I did not believe a word of Thackeray's story and felt that he was taking advantage of my sister's sympathetic nature.

'Catherine,' said Thackeray, ignoring me. 'Though everyone called her Cathy.'

'Oh . . .' began Cathy, all flustered.

'Mr Thackeray is teasing you, Cathy,' I said, making it clear by my expression that I thought that his behaviour towards my sister was unacceptable.

'I assure you I am not,' said Thackeray. 'Cathy was her name, I promise you.'

'I'm not sure what to make of your "promises", Thackeray,' I said. 'If that is your name.'

'Ethan, Ethan,' he said, with his arms outstretched. 'You have no fight with me. If I have said anything to offend you – or Miss Cathy here – then I apologise. I am no longer used to polite conversation. I have been too long away from ... *ordinary* people.'

I raised an eyebrow and grimaced at the stress Thackeray placed on the word 'ordinary', but I let it pass without comment.

'I'm sure you haven't offended anyone,' said Cathy, frowning at me. 'And if anyone is being impolite it is my brother.'

I told Cathy in no uncertain terms that I thought she was being unfair and we quickly became embroiled in the kind of enthusiastic bickering well known to siblings all over the world. We had barely begun when we were interrupted by our guest banging on the table with the flat of his hand.

'Ethan, Miss Cathy! I should not want to be the cause of any argument. No more cross words now.'

Cathy turned up her nose and arched an eyebrow haughtily and turned away from me. I countered this with a grunt and a shrug. Thackeray beamed, looking happier than he had the entire time he had been in our company. I rather resented the pleasure he seemed to be taking in Cathy and I falling out, however briefly.

'Come, let's leave that squall behind us and sail on. Who's for a new story?' he said, rubbing his hands together.

'Yes, please,' said Cathy, nose and eyebrow

descending slowly. 'What is it about?'

'Well now, have you ever heard of scrimshaw?'

'Of course', I said, eager to disabuse him of the notion he seemed to have gained that we were mere ignorant children. 'It is the name given to the decorative carving in whale teeth and the like.'

'Aye', said Thackeray, nodding and leaning forward. 'So it is. Well, my next story concerns just such a piece of work.'

The Scrimshaw Imp

Edward Salter was walking back to his ship, waiting in the harbour at Alexandria. He had become separated from his fellow crewmen, who were all older than he, and while he had been fascinated by the exotic sights and sounds of the city, it was dark now and he had become fearful of being alone.

As Edward walked the long, poorly lit quay, a little nervous of the shadows, he saw ahead that someone was lying prone on the cobbles.

He had been brought up to believe that you should not walk by someone in distress but should help your fellow man if you're able, and so he ran towards the figure. As he approached, Edward was shocked to see that the man looked as though he had been mauled by a lion or a bear, his clothes ripped, as was the flesh beneath, his bones clearly broken, his head crushed like a melon, his face horribly reshaped and ruined. Incredibly, though, the man was still alive.

'Who did this?' said Edward, bending over him.

The man groaned pitifully but made no reply. Edward could see someone walking away further along the quayside – another sailor it looked like. He almost called out, but, looking again at the man on the ground, thought twice and kept his peace.

The injured man was holding something in a ruined hand, and with all his remaining strength – for it was clear his life was ebbing away – he tried to hurl it towards the sea. It skittered over the cobbles and came to rest a yard or so from the edge.

He motioned for Edward to come closer, and this he did. The man grabbed his jacket and tried to speak, but though he moved his mouth no sound other than a strangulated choking emerged, and within seconds his grip loosened and he slumped lifeless to the ground.

Had he been at home in London Edward might have sought out a constable, or called for help. But he was not at home. He was a sailor in a foreign land with a mutilated corpse at his feet.

In that instant he decided that he could do no more to help the man. He had not seen the attacker and could not assist in his capture. Better by far that he return to his ship. But as he was walking away, curiosity got the better of him.

Edward was intrigued to discover what it was that the dead man had been so determined to throw into the water. He walked over and picked the object up, and almost as soon as he did so he heard voices. They were a long way off, but even so he did not want to be found there and, putting the thing in his pocket, he walked briskly away.

Once back on the *Buck*, Edward turned it over in his hand. It was a whale tooth – a big one, from the jaws of a great sperm whale no doubt – and etched into the surface was some kind of picture. Edward could not see what the picture showed because the light was too poor, but he could see that it was done with that odd mixture of crudeness and intensity that gave such pieces their strange charm. He certainly was glad it had not ended up in the harbour.

Edward went below deck. An old mariner called Morton, who had no interest in carousing ashore and little remaining curiosity for foreign ports, was sitting on a barrel, reading a book by lantern light. His eyes were failing and he was using a magnifying glass. Taking the scrimshaw tooth from his pocket, Edward asked Morton if he could borrow it.

Morton agreed and Edward held the tooth near a lantern and peered through the glass, marvelling again at the astonishing complexity and intricacy of the carving.

One side of the tooth carried a depiction of a quayside, along which was walking a sailor. Behind the figure was a tall building with ochre walls, a terracotta tiled roof and a tall castellated clock tower on which there was a weathervane in the shape of an arrow.

When he turned the tooth over, Edward found another carved scene, this time showing a three-masted sailing ship, much like the *Buck*, in a harbour much like Alexandria. Along the curve of the tooth, below the picture, were some words written in a neat, if a little awkward, sloping italic script. They read:

Behold and beware the Scrimshaw Imp.
Behold and beware thy self.

To his amazement, when he held the magnifying glass closer over the skillfully etched ship, he could

see clearly that it was not merely *like* the Buck –
the name on the side stated very clearly that it *was*
the Buck.

Was the owner of the scrimshaw tooth trying to
get to the Buck? Edward had never seen him
before, he was sure of that. Perhaps he had sailed
aboard the ship in the past. Perhaps he was the
artist.

Edward turned the tooth over again, and had
another look at the side showing the sailor on the
quayside. He noticed something he had not seen
before. On the right-hand side of the image, further
along the quayside, was another, far less distinct
figure.

The skill of the scrimshaw artist seemed to have
deserted him in this depiction, for where the first
figure was all detail, down to the buttons on his
jacket and the neckerchief about his throat, the second figure seemed vague and blurred, as if caught
in the act of movement. The maker had clearly not
been satisfied by his work because he had tried to
scratch the figure out. Edward suddenly had a
vision of the injured man and shivered.

He was about to put the tooth in his trunk when
he stared again at the picture engraved on its surface. Though common sense and reason told him it

was impossible, he had the strongest possible impression that the blurry figure had moved. Where it had once occupied a space at the far right of the tooth, it was now further to the left and distinctly closer to the sailor.

Edward peered at the space where the figure had been, but there was no sign of a mark; the surface of the tooth was untouched and as smooth as silk. He must have been mistaken. And yet he knew in the pit of his stomach that he was not.

As Edward sat there staring at the scrimshaw tooth, old Morton stepped over to see what was the cause of his troubled expression.

'What's that you have, boy?' he asked, and then seeing the tooth in Edward's hand, said, 'Ah – 'tis a piece of scrimshaw work, and a fine one too, by the looks of it.'

He asked to take a closer look, and Edward passed it to him, calmed by being brought back to normality. Already, with Morton beside him, the possibility that he had simply misremembered the image seemed the more likely explanation than that it had somehow moved.

'Did you do this?' said Morton.

'Me?' said Edward. 'No. I have no skill in such things. It was . . . given to me.'

'That's quite a gift,' said Morton. 'That's the *Buck* and no mistake. What does it say there? It's too small for my eyes.'

Edward told him. Morton sucked the air between his teeth with a whistle.

'What do you think it means?' said Edward.

'I don't know,' said Morton. 'I don't like the sound of it though. You say someone gave it to you? Who?'

Edward licked his lips and looked at the floor.

'I . . . in a way, I found it.'

'Did you – in a way – steal it?' asked Morton.

'No!' said Edward. 'Not really . . .'

With a big sigh, Edward told Morton what had happened: about the injured man and the scrimshaw tooth. Morton shook his head.

'There's something bad here,' he said, turning over the tooth. 'This figure,' he went on, seeing Edward's confusion. 'Supposing that's you. It looks like you, come to think of it.'

Edward had noticed that already, but then, with its neckerchief, jacket and trousers, it could have been any sailor.

'And what about that figure following behind?' continued Morton.

'Following?' said Edward, though he knew it was

true. He could not bring himself to tell Morton that it also appeared to move.

'Maybe that's the Scrimshaw Imp', said Morton, handing the tooth back. 'Maybe that's what you have to beware.'

The thought of such a thing following him any-where made Edward's guts clench and troubled his sleep when he eventually lay back in his bunk and closed his eyes. He opened them five hours later to find Morton looking into his face.

'Get rid of it, lad', he said, pointing to the tooth, which lay on top of Edward's bunk. 'Get rid of it if you know what's good for you. There's sorcery in it. Take a hammer to it, lad. Smash the thing and be done.'

Morton was already going before Edward had fully come to his wits, but he knew there was some-thing in what the old man had said. He followed Morton up and out on to the deck just as the call came out that they were setting sail.

Edward walked to the side of the ship and took the scrimshaw tooth from his pocket. The eerie light of daybreak shimmered across its surface and gave it an even more unearthly quality. The whale tooth took on a weird lustre, as if lit from within.

The little boats of local traders and fishermen

clogged the harbour. They had all made their last attempts to sell their wares to the foreigners and now they watched them leave, readying themselves for a new ship and new customers. A boy on a nearby fishing boat waved and Edward waved absent-mindedly back at him.

Morton was right, he thought. No good could come of keeping such a thing. It was bewitched in some way, he was sure of it. It had clearly done the previous owner no good, a fact acknowledged by the dying man's desire to get rid of the thing. Perhaps Edward should do what that man was trying to do but could not.

Edward held the scrimshaw tooth over the side of the ship and let go, letting it fall into the shimmering sea. It struck the water, point down, with barely a splash, and Edward walked away, feeling as if whatever spell the tooth had cast over his life was now ended.

He had not taken two steps, however, before he was overcome by the strangest sensation. He felt suddenly cold, despite the heat of the morning, but worse – far worse than that – he could not breathe.

Edward choked and reached for his throat, feeling for some blockage but knowing that the sensation was different. It felt as though the very air he was trying to breathe had become solid; as if, instead of air, he was swallowing water.

Edward staggered back to the side of the ship and looked at where the tooth had fallen in.

The Egyptian boy on the fishing boat had seen the whole scene, and while he had found Edward's behaviour baffling – as he did so much of the behaviour of these foreigners – he had an eye for an opportunity and, speculating that the sailor might be pleased to have whatever it was he had dropped returned to him, he dived into the water and emerged, waving the tooth in the air.

As soon as the tooth was above the water, the air flooded back into Edward's lungs. He leaned over the rail, coughing and thanking the boy profusely and waving for him to bring the tooth aboard.

Edward gave the breathless, smiling boy a handful of coins – more money than the boy might normally see in a year – and sent him back to his father aboard the fishing boat, where they both waved back at the crazy Englishman with broad grins.

Edward acknowledged them, but he could not share their smiles. His fate seemed to have become entangled with that of the tooth he held once more in his shaking hand. He thought of Morton's exhortation to 'take a hammer to the thing' and felt a shudder run through his body.

Looking at the carvings again, he saw that in the image of the Buck the ship was preparing to set sail – just as the actual ship was. The fishing boat was also shown, father and son waving. And there was a sailor at the gunwales, waving back. Edward stared wide-eyed; was his life being mirrored in the scrimshaw tooth, or was it being determined by it, *controlled* by it?

If so, was he doomed then to stand idly by as a spectator while his destiny was made a puppet to this infernal creation? But what could he do? He clearly could not destroy the thing, but neither could he discard it, for who knew what accident might befall it, and what effect that could have on his life?

No – he would have to keep it by him at all times and take especial care of it. Perhaps, when he had calmed a little and understood more of its power, he might glean something that would provide an escape route from its grip.

And so the Buck sailed on, moving west along the Mediterranean and calling at the port of Naples, one of half a dozen stops they would make before heading home to London. Vesuvius reared up behind the city, smoke still belching belligerently from its cone after one of its frequent eruptions.

As they moored Edward looked at the volcano in the distance, and the idea that it might at any moment explode into violent life, showering rock and ash down on the city, struck a chord with him. He felt able now to appreciate something of the nature of living in the shadow of such a monster. Perhaps the secret was in accepting his fate as the Neapolitans had done. Perhaps the scrimshaw tooth really did show him what would happen in any case, no matter what choices he made. Perhaps he had never been as free as he thought.

Edward took the scrimshaw tooth from his pocket and turned it over in his hand, feeling again the weight of it, the smoothness of the untouched areas, the texture of the incised drawing.

He looked at the image of the *Buck* and saw – as he knew he would – that the ship was in the Bay of Naples, with Vesuvius scratched into the background. He registered this with a calmness that surprised him. Was it possible, after all, that even something as dark and strange as this could be accepted?

He did not look at the drawing of the sailor. He did not find that image so easy to accept. The scene with the ship seemed simply to reflect what he could see around him and, miraculous though that evolving drawing was, it did at least have its roots in the world he knew.

The drawing of the sailor and the thing that followed him – the Scrimshaw Imp, he supposed – portrayed a mystery, and a mystery that troubled him both in its inscrutability and in the sinister nature of what it illustrated.

Edward's mind was still buzzing with questions as he stepped ashore. What was it that the picture represented? Did it show an actual event or was it symbolic in some way? What did it mean? Was it a warning? Was the scrimshaw tooth signalling danger or luring him towards some kind of unknown and unknowable peril? Then, all at once, as if in answer to these questions, he looked around and noticed for the first time where he was.

A sense of dread numbed his entire body as he gradually recognised the scene around him. He felt like he had when the scrimshaw tooth had been dropped in the ocean. He felt as though he were drowning.

This was the quayside depicted on the scrimshaw tooth. There was the tall ochre building with the clock tower, the pantiled roof and the arrow-shaped weathervane. One of his crewmates was up ahead. He had an urge to call to him, to tell

him of the dread that was mounting in his heart – but how could he? He would sound deranged.

It seemed utterly incongruous that on a day such as that day – with the sun high in a cobalt sky, with seabirds crying and fishermen singing as they brought their catch ashore – that on a day like that there could be something so dark and from the sunless world of shadows so near.

And yet he knew with every fibre of his being that the thing from the scrimshaw tooth, the Scrimshaw Imp, whatever it was, was there. If he turned now he would see it, the shadow-thing, and the fear and dread of seeing the terrible vagueness of it was almost unbearable. He could feel its breath on the back of his neck.

In desperation Edward took out a clasp knife and, opening it with shaking hands, he began to gouge and scrape away at the image of the Scrimshaw Imp on the tooth. Why had he not thought of this before? He felt a giddying sense of triumph. In seconds, all that was left of the shadowy form was a collection of deep scratches. Then the pain began.

Every inch of his body was aflame with agony. Blood was pouring from him, dripping on to the scrimshaw tooth and the cobbles. His legs would no longer support him and he fell to the ground. As he lay there, his life draining away, he could see his arms and hands were slashed and scratched as if by some giant blade, and he knew he was not the *sailor* in the picture. He was the Scrimshaw Imp.

Edward's vision blurred . . . He became aware of a face, of someone leaning towards him, asking him who he was and what had happened. The face was full of horror at the sight of such injuries. It was the expression his face must have worn in Alexandria.

With his dying breaths he tried to warn the sailor, who even now was picking up the scrimshaw tooth. But his mouth would no longer answer the brain's call, and was so entirely ruined that were it still connected it could not have formed the words.

Just as Edward had, the sailor saw that there was nothing he could do and, not wanting trouble, he chose to leave. The last thing Edward saw, as he lay with one ragged ear to the ground, was the image of the sailor stopping to look at the scrimshaw tooth, putting it in his pocket and walking on.

'Ethan,' said Cathy, 'you're hurting.'

I had been holding Cathy's hand to comfort her during the story, because I could see she had been unduly frightened by it from the very start. But the tale had clearly had an effect on me also, for I was now crushing my poor sister's hand as every muscle in my body contracted with dread.

As always, Thackeray looked mightily pleased to have caused such a reaction in us and again I had to fight the urge to punch him on the nose. Outside, the storm was easing and there was a welcome calm about the headland and our inn. The branches at the window had ceased their fidgeting and clawing.

'It seems the storm has had its fill of us,' said Thackeray. 'My ship will return soon and I will be on my way, and you good folks will have the place to yourselves once more. I thank you kindly for your hospitality.'

'You are very welcome,' said Cathy. 'I wish you would stay and meet our father.'

'Mr Thackeray does not want to meet Father, Cathy,' I said. 'He must not keep his ship waiting – whatever ship that is.'

I said this last in a particular tone that I hoped would signify that I personally doubted that he was even a sailor and was more likely some sort of vagabond or con man.

'Is there something you want to say, friend?' he said.

'Only that I still wonder at how you came to be here on such a night,' I said. 'The weather has been far too wild for any ship to reach the harbour. How is that you came ashore?'

'I swam,' he said.

'Very funny,' I said. 'But I wonder why you do not wish to say.'

Thackeray closed his eyes and shook his head slowly. When he opened them he looked at Cathy, and when he spoke his voice was cool and quiet. The wind had dropped as if in response, and there seemed to be a hush of expectancy in the air.

'Storms are part of a sailor's life,' said Thackeray, 'and every mariner, from fisherman to admiral, has his mettle tested some time or other. Storms come and go. A ship like mine would not normally be troubled by them. But some storms are exceptionally powerful. Such was this one.'

I opened my mouth to interrupt him, but there was something about his expression that made me think better of it.

'Perhaps I was distracted by the proximity to the place where I was born and spent my tender years. Perhaps I was thinking about Cathy and the life we might have had. Perhaps I was looking towards this very inn perched up here on the clifftop.'

He took a drink and slowly lowered the empty glass.

'Whatever the cause', he said, 'I did not see the wave that knocked me overboard.'

'Goodness!' said Cathy. 'You were thrown into the sea in that storm? How did you survive, Mr Thackeray?'

'Yes, Mr Thackeray', I said with a raised eyebrow. 'How *did* you escape drowning?'

As usual he ignored me and addressed Cathy instead.

'Time and again the rolling waves crashed over me and dragged me under, but each time I surfaced again. I saw the inn on the cliff and knew that I was heading towards the shore. In no time I was standing in the surf in the bay at the base of these cliffs.'

'And how did you get from there to here?' I asked. 'The cliffs are high and treacherous.'

'I climbed', he said calmly.

'You climbed?' I laughed.

'Ethan!' chided Cathy.

'I cannot tell you what to believe', said Thackeray, sitting back in his chair. 'I can only tell you what occurred.'

The storm was over now and there was a silence such as I had never known before. The sea had ceased its roar and the gulls their crying. Thackeray looked down at the table, his face veiled by shadow.

'I knew this inn as a boy,' he began, without looking up, 'in happier days. I thought that I might see it one more time.'

He seemed so sincere in these reflections that I had to remind myself that he can only have been a few years my senior. If he had been here often enough to have grown sentimental about it, I would have remembered him. Cathy was clearly having the same difficulty, despite her desire to believe in this strange visitor.

'But we would have been here when you came,' she said. 'I may have been so young as to have forgotten – though I am known for my good memory – but Ethan would surely have some recollection, what with you both being boys. Don't you remember us?'

There was a pause. 'It was all a long time ago,' he said quietly, 'as I have said. Such things and the memories of them are the wake a life leaves at its passing.'

I am a little ashamed to say I took some satisfaction in seeing Thackeray struggle to come up with any sensible explanation, and in seeing the look of disappointment that clearly showed on my sister's face.

'The storm has blown over, Cathy', I said. 'Mr Thackeray should be going.'

'Ethan is right, Miss Cathy', Thackeray said, standing up. 'I must be on my way.' He gave me another of his patronising smiles.

'But surely your "ship" will be long gone, Mr Thackeray', I said, unable to resist the temptation to pick further at the fabric of his tale.

'She will come for me soon enough', said Thackeray. 'She is not a ship to leave her crew behind.'

He smiled and moved towards the door. But he had barely left the table when Cathy grabbed him by the arm, surprising me and herself by her boldness.

'Oh please, Mr Thackeray', she said in her most pleading voice. 'Please, please, please. One more story before you go.'

I sighed loudly, glaring at Cathy, but she paid no heed.

'But I thought my last tale frightened you, Miss Cathy', said Thackeray.

'So it did', she said with a giggle. 'But I do so

love to be frightened!'

Thackeray grinned and, to my dismay, sat back down.

'Very well, then, Miss Cathy,' he said. 'One more story. Just for you.'

The Black Ship

The ship had been becalmed for more than two days. Not the merest breath of wind blew. The wide flat ocean stretched itself out to north and south, as black and limpid as a barrel of pitch under the cold night sky.

Now, to the city dweller and the farmer there is nothing especially ominous about a still night; far from it. The quiet means that their sleep will be untroubled and filled with peaceful dreaming.

But a sailing man is made of different stuff. He needs to feel the roll of the ship beneath his feet. He wants to hear the creak of taut rigging and the crackle of sailcloth filled to bursting.

Without wind in its canvas, without waves on the sea, a sailing ship becomes imprisoned, trapped as if by ice. That thing of beauty which can transport you to the four corners of the world becomes in windless weather a sad and useless beast.

Time was becalmed along with the ship, and to bide away those long hours of inactivity some of the mariners crowded into the captain's cabin to tell tales, for no man loves a story more than a sailor, either in the telling or the hearing.

The men sat around the long map table. The low curved ceiling was ribbed with beams. A leaded window opened out on to the ship's stern. A lantern was the only illumination in the cabin.

This lantern was the temporary property of each storyteller in turn, meaning that while the tale was in progress the audience sat silently focused on the grimly uplit face of the storyteller.

Jacob the cabin boy poured the captain another drink and stood back, listening to the stories. Gibson, a thick set and surly man hailing from the coast of Northumberland, was telling his tale, the lantern shining in his face, his gold tooth twinkling as he spoke.

'We struck the reef at night,' he growled. 'The

sound was something terrible to hear. The timbers cracked and split like they was being chewed by some great monster. As she was going down, a mighty wave slapped into her and broke her in two.

'Men were falling into the sea every which way. You could hear them shouting and calling, their voices filled with that fear a sailor has in his voice when his ship is shot from under him.

'The lucky men drowned there and then, God bless their souls, and died good sailors' deaths, taken down deep to the ocean bed to rest alongside their ship.

'Those of us afloat could now see there was an island beyond the reef. It was a long way off but it was a hope and I was a strong swimmer. But no sooner had I made my first move than I heard the screams.

'Men ahead of me were being forced by the waves on to the reef as they swam. Some of you know those reefs. Those reefs are jagged with coral and spiked with shells. They can rip the flesh from you in minutes.

'One after another of my shipmates was thrown against that infernal reef to be chewed and gnawed by it, while I, for the luck of being that much further out to sea, floated in the blackness, listening to their death throes.

'As dawn came I could see the island clearly, but just as clearly I saw that I would never be able to reach it, for the reef spread out far beyond my view, barring my way.

'Clearly, too, I could see the sport it had had with my shipmates. Floating between the reef and me was a sight no man should have to see: a stinking soup of flesh and blood that would have made a butcher puke.

'The first fin flashed by me so close I felt the watery draft of the shark's passing. Within minutes there were a dozen. I had thought all the crew were dead until the sharks began to feed, but then the screaming began again. Mercifully, it did not last long.

'An old sea dog told me once that sharks come to movement like they come to blood and that the thing to do is to keep still. So that's what I tried to do, though I had to tread water to stop myself drifting on to the reef.

'The sharks gorged themselves and I saw smaller fish move in to pick the bones while sea birds flew in, squawking, dropping to the water and flying off with some vile piece of meat hanging from their beaks.

'When they had had their fill, the sharks began to leave, their fins cutting through the water like black-sailed schooners. One after another they glided by. One even brushed against me as it did so and I felt the sleek leather of its skin against my hand.

'The last shark turned to swim away and I was pleased to see that it took a route past me at some distance. But as it came level with me it hesitated and changed direction. It swam slowly past my legs. I saw its terrible soulless eye roll back and then it turned and took my ribs in its jaws and bit deep.

'I could not cry out for the pain of it, but I somehow still had the wits to pull my knife from its sheath at my side and I stabbed the beast with all my strength. It rolled away with a piece of me in its jaws and my knife in its head.

'Now I was bleeding and still had no way of getting to the island. Sooner or later the sharks would return; I only hoped I would be dead before they came.'

'I swear those sharks take a bigger piece of you every time you tell this tale, Gibson,' said Finch, a skinny Cornishman.

Most of the crew laughed and Gibson blushed a

little and then laughed along with them. Jacob saw his chance and grabbed the lantern.

'I've got a tale, if you've the guts to hear it!'

One or two of the sailors snorted and signalled to him to put the lantern back.

'Come, lad', said one. 'This is men's business. Listen if you've a mind to, but leave the tale-telling to them as have a tale to tell. Besides, Gibson here hasn't finished.'

'Let the boy tell his tale', said Finch. 'We know Gibson's story well enough. We could do with a new one!'

'Aye', said Gibson, slapping Jacob on the back. 'Let him speak if wants to.'

Several sailors grumbled noisily, but Jacob grabbed a stool and sat himself down at the table. The lantern lit up his face and threw a giant's shadow on the curved cabin ceiling.

'Pipe down now, lads', said the captain. 'As I see it, if young Jacob has a tale, then he's as much right to tell it as any man here. Go on, son, sing out.'

'Well', said Jacob, 'the tale I tell was told to me by the cook on a brig I served on about a year past. This cook – Dawson was his name – he worked on a merchant ship sailing out of Bristol, bound for the Spice Islands.'

'The ship was a fine one with a good captain, and they made good time, rounding the Hope without a care. Then, when they thought they were safe and they were near their destination, a fearful storm blew up with waves like mountains with foaming white peaks.

'The captain and crew they did their best, but the storm was too great. It downed the mainmast like it was a twig and crippled the ship, and then a mighty wave hit like an axe and broke her in two. All the crew were drowned.

'All, that is, except this sea-cook, Dawson, who had managed to reach a piece of the mainmast and had held on for dear life throughout the raging of the storm.

'When the storm ended, Dawson found himself afloat among the wreckage of his ship and the dead of the crew. He called out for survivors but no answer came.

'How many days Dawson clung to that mast he never could say, but however terrible the days were, with the sun beating down on him like a hammer, the nights were worse, knowing that he was surrounded by miles of empty black ocean with only the bloated, floating dead of his shipmates for company.

'Then, one day, a fog rolled in across the sea. It came upon him so sudden-like and thick that, though it meant some respite from the sun, it filled him with dread.

'And all at once he heard it: the wonderful sound of water slapping against timbers, the rustle and flap of sailcloth. It was a ship! Rescue was at hand!

'Sure enough, the faint shape of masts and sails hove into view through the mist, becoming darker and darker all the while. Dawson's heart rose up like a bird and tears of joy ran down his sun-cracked face.

'But then, as he was about to raise his arm aloft and sing out for help, his attention was distracted by a movement in the water nearby. A body that had kept grim company with him those past few days, face down and floating some two feet away, twitched.'

'Twitched, you say?' said the ship's carpenter.

'Aye,' said Jacob. 'Twitched. At first Dawson thought his eyes had tricked him, that the sun had taken its toll on his mind – but no; the body twitched again. There could be no doubt this time.

'Then all at once the body lifted itself up, water dripping from its lank black hair, and raised its arms and waved. Dawson stared in horror. There was no way that the man could be alive. He had not moved for days. In any event, the cry that escaped his lips was one that no living man might make, the sea gurgling in his lifeless throat more like a bilge pump than a human voice.

'Then Dawson saw another body lift itself – and another – and another – until half a dozen corpses waved and cried out like hideous mermen, their faces all pale and soft, like fish that have been pickled in brine.

'Dawson looked to the ship, his need for rescue all the more urgent for being surrounded by these living corpses of his fellows.

'He was about to call out, but saw that the crew were already helping aboard a man he knew to be as dead as a marlinspike. Not only did they show no horror at his appearance, they greeted him most warmly as if he were an old friend.

'Dawson looked at the ship with new eyes and saw its true form. The timbers were black, holed and rotted so near the waterline that there was no godly way that the ship could stay afloat.

'The masts were likewise black, rotted and cracked, eaten by worms and bored by beetles. The sails were frayed and thin, as flimsy as a fly's wing.

'As the crew of the ship helped another of the

floating dead aboard, Dawson realised that this was the Black Ship that mariners spoke of, crewed by the corpses of shipwrecked seamen.

'Though the thought of another minute in that briny waste filled him with horror, Dawson grabbed the mast with both hands and submerged himself as the ship approached. He saw its rotten planks pass by beneath the water as he held his breath and prayed that they would not see him.

'When he finally burst to the surface, the ship was gone and the fog with it. All the corpses of his crewmates were gone, too. He was alone once more and half mad with what he'd seen.

'Dawson had given up all hope when another ship appeared on the horizon, and he was rescued and brought back to Bristol, where he vowed never to sail again – a vow he broke within the year, knowing no other life than that of the sea. In time he came to serve as cook aboard a Royal Navy ship-of-the-line – a ship on which I also served – and there, one night, he told the tale I have now told to you.'

Though he had not been sure what reaction he might get from the hardened sea dogs round the table, Jacob had not expected the total silence that greeted the end of his tale.

No man spoke and though every eye was turned to Jacob, the faces did not show fear or amusement, but were instead wearing strange and melancholy expressions.

'Now, then', said Jacob, banging his fist down on the table. 'Was that a tale or no?'

'Aye, lad', said the captain, but still no one else spoke nor moved.

'What is it?' said Jacob. 'Do you not believe the tale? I swear I heard it from Dawson's own lips and he was a man who was not given to foolish talk.'

'Aye', said the captain. 'Every man here knows of the Black Ship.'

'Well, then', said Jacob, noticing for the first time that fog was curling in through the open window.

'How came you to serve on this ship, Jacob?' said the captain.

It struck Jacob as an odd question for the captain to ask, as it must have been he who granted him leave to serve aboard his ship. All the same, for some strange reason, Jacob could not remember how he came to be there.

'Wreck ahoy!' came a voice. The captain stood up with a sigh.

'Look lively, lads', he said. 'There's work to do.'

'Aye aye, Captain', they responded and rose as one

to go out on to the deck.

It was then that Jacob noticed with horror that Gibson had a huge piece of his side missing. His clothes hung down limply, mercifully covering, though only just, what must have been a massive bite-shaped wound.

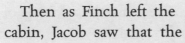

Then as Finch left the cabin, Jacob saw that the ragged hole in his cap now glowed with the milky light coming from the open door. The hole passed completely through his head. The captain saw the expression on Jacob's face and smiled grimly.

'Think, lad,' he said. 'Do you not remember how you came aboard?'

Jacob tried to remember, closing his eyes to help, but his mind seemed filled with the same fog that encircled the ship. Then it came back to him all at once: the French frigate off Gibraltar, the grapeshot whistling past, the mainmast crashing to the deck, the sound of cannon blast and the howls of the dying, and the musket ball that broke his ribs above his heart and snuffed out the candle of his life. He put his hand to his jacket and let his finger explore the hole.

The ship had gone down, taking most men with it, including Dawson, sucked down into the slimy depths of the ocean, where crabs grew fat on the glut of food. He alone had floated free, as if in a dream, and it was he alone who had answered the Black Ship's call.

'Come, lad,' said the captain. 'Let us meet our new shipmates.'

There was a great suffocating silence as Thackeray finished his story, as if we were all now in the hold of a sunken ship and the sounds of the dry world were muffled by submerged ears. The raucous clamour of the storm had died away, and its breath was now a sigh, now a whisper.

'You can't say *that* tale was true,' I said, trying to assuage my own fear by a forced return to the rational. 'How could anyone be dead and not know it and how could you know what goes on aboard the Black Ship, if such a vessel exists?'

'Well, now,' he said with a smile. 'I think you

know the answer to those questions.'

I certainly had not expected such a reply and after a moment I assured him that I did not, and Cathy grabbed my sleeve.

'What does he mean, Ethan?' she asked nervously.

'He is trying to frighten us, Cathy,' I said. 'They are only yarns, and I am afraid that Mr Thackeray does not know when to stop.'

Thackeray looked at us both, but his smile seemed now tinged with sadness. I saw something that looked very much like pity in his eyes, and I resented it.

'Why do you look at us in that way?' I asked, standing up and making clear that I meant to knock him down if he did not give me a satisfactory answer.

'Calm yourself, friend,' he said. 'I meant no harm.'

'Perhaps it is time that you finally left, Mr Thackeray,' I said coldly. 'The storm seems to have passed.'

Thackeray took a deep breath and sighed. This time there was no objection from Cathy.

'Aye. It's time I was going,' he said, getting to his feet. 'My fate lies elsewhere.'

A bell sounded some way off in the distance, like

a church bell but with an unearthly resonance that seemed to vibrate in my very bones and which made the glass on the table hum to its tune.

'My ship is calling,' said Mr Thackeray, 'and I must answer. So I bid you adieu. Ethan, Miss Cathy – 'twas a pleasure to meet you both.'

'Mr Thackeray,' I said, but I did not shake his hand.

''Twas an honour to meet you too,' said Cathy, blushing in a most annoying way, and I noted that she seemed to flutter her eyelashes. 'Thank you for telling us so many stories.'

'My pleasure,' he said, gazing at her with a haunted expression. And Thackeray finally walked away towards the door with Cathy and I following close behind.

He opened the door and stood on the threshold for a while, gazing out into the night. He seemed annoyingly reluctant to actually leave, and I was sorely tempted to shove him out and bolt the door behind him. In any event, he turned and bowed to Cathy and to me, and, with one last twinkling smile, he set off towards the cliff edge as though he were about to throw himself off.

Cathy let out a little shriek as he made no attempt to stop himself but did indeed step over the edge, and we ran to see what had become of him. To our amazement he was sliding and hopping down the sheer cliff face with the agility and sure-footedness of a mountain goat. He reached the bottom in seconds and stepped nonchalantly on to the rocks and sand of the bay as if he did this kind of thing every day.

The great heavy mass of cloud that had blanketed the night sky and hidden every star from view now parted theatrically from east to west, like the curtains at a music hall, and there, taking centre stage in the bay, was a three-masted sailing ship, spot-lit by a milk-white moon.

A boat was rowing ashore from the anchored ship to meet him. There was something so dream-like and unearthly about the scene that it was a little while before I began to see the detail of it.

The moon was near full and as bright as a beacon. I squinted at the ship and at the boat, trying to make sense of what the spectral light was telling me.

The hull of the ship seemed to be holed like a moth-eaten coat, the moonlit sea clearly visible through its pierced ribs. The sails were furled but seemed tattered and frayed. In fact the whole ship looked worm-eaten and rotten to the rib-timbers.

I assumed that this damage was as a result of the tempest, but the more I looked, the less this explanation seemed to hold true. The ship appeared to be corrupted by the ravages of time more than by the actions of the weather.

There was something equally ragged about the crew of the rowing boat that neared the shore and of the crew that was visible standing at the gunwales and who were silhouetted among the rigging.

As the boat reached the shore, Thackeray grabbed a line that was tossed to him, waded into the sea and nimbly jumped aboard, helped by hands and arms that seemed not to possess the prerequisite amount of flesh. A thought had wormed its way into my head, but it was Cathy who gave voice to it.

'That's the Black Ship, isn't it?' she said, and, though I dearly wanted to reply that such a notion was childish nonsense, my security in the rational world had taken flight and I could not bring myself to say the words.

For I knew in my heart that it was true.

'And if that's the Black Ship, then . . .' Cathy did not finish the sentence, but there was no need to. If that was the Black Ship, then our storyteller, just like the crew who now crawled over the ship like spiders, unfurling the sails and hauling up the anchor, was dead.

Wolfsbane

Cathy and I watched the Black Ship sail away, dissolving into a fog that had mysteriously built up on the horizon. So Thackeray had been telling the truth. He could not drown in the storm because he was already dead – already drowned most like, as he had no signs of injury. The cliffs held no fear for him. What had he to fear, after all?

We returned slowly to the inn and, once inside, the hypnotic strangeness of the moonlit bay, the ragged ship and its ragged crew, the storyteller and his fearful yarns – they all seemed to retreat from view like a nightmare does to the waking dreamer who, when asked what it was that woke him so afraid, can recall only the fear itself and not the cause.

And as this spectral world retreated, the real world and its concerns came flooding back, and with them the realisation that our father had still not returned. I could see that Cathy was worried and I put my arm around her shoulder to reassure her.

We went back to the settles by the fire, where we had so recently been listening to Thackeray's sea tales. His empty glass still sat on the table. His strange aura clung to the place with such vivid persistence that we both found ourselves staring at the space he had vacated as if he might materialise in front of our very eyes. I shook my head, still troubled by his visit. Why had he been drawn to our inn? Why did he not go and haunt his childhood home, and where was that exactly?

It struck me then that if Thackeray really was dead, we did not have any way of knowing how long ago his death occurred. His uniform was old-fashioned. That must be why we had not heard of any Thackerays living nearby. Thackeray, his family, his sweetheart Cathy, were all from the past, how distant though I did not know.

But I needed to shake off the enchantment of Thackeray's visit, if such a thing were possible, to look to the present and address the all too real predicament we had been so long distracted from.

The first faint gleaming of the new dawn would soon be appearing in the east and I told Cathy that since we were fully recovered from whatever had ailed us, we would at first light, if Father had still not returned, make our way down to the village.

The storm had passed now and whatever our father had said about staying where we were, we could hardly be expected to sit there and do nothing. I had wanted to believe that his act in racing out into the teeth of the storm to try to find help for his sick children was a turning point in our lives. He had gone away from us over the past years with his drinking and evil temper, and strangely, despite his physical absence, he felt closer to us than he had for a long, long time. But I began to wonder now if he had not simply deserted us.

Cathy readily agreed with me that we should leave the inn at daybreak. Like me, she felt the need to *do* something. Thackeray's tales, however unsettling, had with their odd intensity fired our spirits and filled us both with a kind of crackling nervous energy.

Suddenly there was someone at the door, rattling the handle. Assuming it to be Father, we ran over, but quickly saw through the window that there were at least two men beyond. Cathy leapt to my side. Had the spectral storyteller returned? Had he brought some of his ghostly crewmates with him? No – it could not be. We had watched the Black Ship sail away.

And yet who could know what such spirits were capable of? He and his grim companions might have flown across the bay like crows or bats. I cannot recall a time I felt so afraid or so unsure of what I knew or trusted that I knew.

For Thackeray was one thing, but the thought of a dozen of those dead-but-somehow-living mariners entering the inn and occupying it with their tattered presence filled me with dread, and I could see that Cathy felt the same. We heard the sound of jangling keys.

But before I could think about a plan of action, the door burst open and I grabbed Cathy's hand and pulled her into an adjoining storeroom, out of sight, praying we had not been seen. Crouching with Cathy at my side, we could peer through the gap between the door and the jamb.

Two men had entered the inn, both young, in

their twenties, and both curiously dressed, wearing trousers as sailors do, though they were like no sailors I had ever seen. Their clothes were well made but of a strange design, as were their hats, which were domes with a narrow brim.

'We are taking something of a risk entering the place,' said one of the men. 'It has been liable to fall into the sea for many years.'

Cathy looked at me and shared my puzzled expression. Who were these men and why did they not call out for assistance? They seemed to assume the inn was empty.

'Do you know I'm sure I felt the building move just then?' he said.

'It is an incredible place,' said the other man. 'But it is deserted you say? It does not *feel* empty.'

Cathy nudged me, but I had already seen it: the man who spoke these words seemed to look straight at us as he did so, as if he knew we were there.

'Well, I assure you it is,' said the other. 'Feel free to look around. We shan't be disturbed.'

They were robbers, I was suddenly certain of it. If they searched they would surely find us, and I decided that it was time to make a move. Thackeray's insinuation that I was not as brave as he for staying here with my family had roused me into recklessness. I stood up and walked into the room to confront them.

'Can I help you, gentlemen?' I said. 'My father has just stepped out for a moment, but will deal with you on his –'

'The locals shun the place completely since the incident,' continued the first man, ignoring me completely.

'Ah yes,' said the other. 'The incident. And it all happened in this very place, Hugh?'

'I must insist!' I said loudly, stepping closer to them with fists clenched, angry beyond words that they should treat me with such utter disdain. Cathy had joined me now.

'Yes,' said the man called Hugh. 'I thought it might amuse you to soak up the atmosphere. I know how fascinated you are by such things, Montague.'

'They can't hear us,' said Cathy. 'Or see us.'

'And it was your father who found them?' said the man called Montague.

'Why can't they see us, Ethan?' said Cathy, frightened and puzzled in equal measure.

'I don't know, Cathy,' I said.

'Yes,' said Hugh. 'And it drove him to an early

grave, I always felt. He never forgave himself.'

'But from what you have told me he had nothing to admonish himself about, said Montague.

'He always felt that he should have been able to tell that the father's drinking had gone beyond the realms of drunkenness and into madness. He was their doctor, after all.' He had tears in his eyes now. 'To poison your own children, Montague . . .' said Hugh. 'What kind of man would do a thing like that?'

'A madman, Hugh,' said Montague, 'as you said.'

'Aye.'

'Make them stop, Ethan,' said Cathy. 'Please make them stop.'

I stepped even closer to the man called Hugh and was about to poke him in the chest, when he turned suddenly and walked towards the settles, where we had listened to Thackeray. He walked straight through me.

'Ethan!' shouted Cathy, grabbing my arm. 'What's happening?' But I did not know. 'Are they ghosts?'

'How did he do it?' said Montague.

'The poison, you mean?' said Hugh. 'It was aconite poisoning.'

'Aconite?' repeated Montague, as if he were making a mental note of every detail.

'Yes', said Hugh. 'It is a common enough plant. *Aconitum napellus*. You might know it as monks-hood or wolfsbane.'

'Wolfsbane? Oh – large spikes of dark blue flowers?'

'That's the one', said Hugh. 'The flowers are pretty enough to be sure, if a little sombre, but the leaves and roots are deadly.'

Montague shook his head. Then I pictured my father manically digging up the flowers in the garden. They were blue. I had a fleeting memory of my mother calling them wolfsbane . . . I must have unwittingly built a wall against these recollections, but it was a wall of sand and the tide was coming in . . .

'They say that the events of that night are played out whenever there is a storm', said Hugh.

'Like the one we have just had?' said Montague, looking, I thought, at Cathy – though of course he could not see her.

'Yes', said Hugh. 'The father poisons his children all over again and leaves them to die while the wind howls around the house. I'm sure it's nonsense.'

Cathy and I stared at each other. I was overcome with a strange sense of knowing these things to be true, of knowing and of forgetting.

'Are you?' said Montague. 'You should try never to be sure of things.'

'You say the strangest things, Montague,' said Hugh with a smile. 'Come on, let's return to the land of the living.'

'Very well,' said Montague, appearing to look at me this time. 'And remind me what happened to the father.'

'Oh, he confessed,' said Hugh. 'Spent the rest of his life in a lunatic asylum. Do you know what's really strange?'

'He poisoned himself?' said Montague.

'Yes, he did,' said Hugh. 'How on earth would you guess a thing like that? He stole some wolfsbane from the cottage garden at the asylum. Would have thought they'd have had more sense than to grow a poisonous plant in a place like that, wouldn't you?'

'Yes,' said Montague with a wry smile.

'It'd be awful if it were true. That the poor beggars – the son and daughter he murdered – if they really did have to go through the thing over and over again.'

'Yes, it would,' said Montague.

'I wonder how a spell like that might be broken?' said Hugh.

'By knowledge,' said Montague. 'Once they know

the truth, they can rest in peace.'

'Let us hope they find the truth, then,' said Hugh.

I reached out and held Cathy's hand and turned to see the tears in her eyes, tears that I shed likewise. But I thought of the Scrimshaw Imp and the horror of being trapped in a grinding wheel of fate. The truth was better than that.

'I say, look at this,' Hugh said.

Montague walked over and Cathy and I followed. Hugh was examining something on the counter and peering up at the ceiling, puzzled.

'What is it?' said Montague.

'Well, look,' said Hugh. 'Look at these old coins here. They're soaking wet, but there is no leak in the ceiling.'

It was the money Thackeray had left.

'And look here.' Hugh walked over to the settles and the table we had so recently vacated. 'Do you see? The seat and floor here are soaking too. Look at these old books.'

Hugh picked up our copy of The Narrative of Arthur Gordon Pym of Nantucket and it fell apart at his touch.

'Leave them be,' said Montague. 'We have imposed ourselves on these children long enough.'

'These children?' said Hugh, raising an eyebrow.

'Oh, the ghost children. I see. Jolly good. Yes, perhaps you're right, Montague. This place gives me the creeps.'

The men walked towards the door and opened it. The first inkling that dawn was about to rise was in the chill night air that entered. At the threshold, Montague turned and, tipping his hat, said quietly, 'Goodbye.' Then the door was closed and we were alone once more. Cathy was the first to speak.

'I think we have waited for Father long enough,' she said. She sounded older somehow.

'Yes, Cathy,' I answered with a sigh. 'I think perhaps you are right.'

'Shall we go up to sleep, then?'

'Yes,' I said, turning to her with a smile.

And so we walked upstairs, hand in hand, the gauze that had once covered our eyes now lifted, and we could see the stars through the holes in the roof above our heads and an owl hooted loudly from the chimney.

We stood together and looked out across the bay, and there in the distance was an inky presence, all black, like the shadow of a ship, and a light winked once from its stern.

'Goodbye, Thackeray,' said Cathy.

'Aye,' I said. 'Goodbye, one and all.'

Cathy lay down on her bed.

'Do you want one last story?' I asked her.

'No,' she said. 'No more stories. I feel so very tired all of a sudden.'

And I felt that tiredness too; it was like the heavy-limbed weariness after a hard day's toil. Sleep seemed like a friend to me now and I was happy to close my eyes and let myself sink into its dark, unfathomable depths.

READ ON

(IF YOU DARE)

FOR SOME SPINE-TINGLING

BONUS STORIES

FATHER

When Cathy and I slipped into our rightful and long-awaited sleep, I had assumed that we would finally be overtaken by blissful oblivion. But it was not to be.

For a while – it is impossible to say how long – it was as though everything was coming to an end and all that we had been in life would soon be gone for ever.

But all at once I felt myself being drawn back up through those black waters until I seemed to break through the surface and, opening my eyes, I saw that we were still in our old room. But now we were not alone.

Looking across the room I saw a figure in the shadows. He was sitting in the chair our mother used to sit in when she told us stories. Despite the bowed head, I knew that it was our father. He looked older, thinner. How many years had he lived on after us?

I was surprised that I still felt afraid – for what could he do to us that he had not already done?

And then I must confess that I took some satisfaction in realising that he too was dead and that whatever curse held us in its grip also held him. I glowered at him as he raised his head to look at me. Why should the dead fear the dead?

'Ethan', he said. 'Son.'

'Why have you come?' I asked coldly. 'What are you doing here?'

'Father!' Cathy cried out suddenly and excitedly. 'I knew you would come back! See, Ethan, it was all a dream!'

But it was no dream.

'Cathy', I said, 'look about you.'

She frowned at my terse voice but she did as I bid. She saw the rotten floorboards, the holes in the ceiling through which snowflakes fell like ash. She saw, too, the miserable, ragged beds we lay upon.

'Oh, Ethan,' she said. 'Is it true, then? Is it true what he did?'

I stared at my father.

'Well?' I said. 'Is it?'

He bowed his head again.

'Yes,' he answered. 'Yes, it is.'

Cathy crept from her bed and sat alongside me. We waited for my father to raise his head once more. His face was pale and his eyes were devoid of all human spark, despite the tears that welled up in them. Had he always looked like this, I wondered.

'Why are you here?' I said again. 'Haven't you caused enough pain?'

'I don't know,' he murmured. 'I was drifting into blackness when I found myself drawn here. I don't know why.'

'There must be some reason,' I said.

He looked at me beseechingly.

'I am so sorry. I was . . .' His voice trailed off.

'Crazed?' I suggested.

'Yes,' he said. 'I was.'

'But not now?'

He shrugged.

'Can the dead be insane? I don't know. I don't feel as though I am. But then I didn't feel insane when I was insane.'

This speech did nothing to put either Cathy or me at ease and I sensed that he wanted to tell us something, and sensed, too, that he perhaps did not know this himself.

'What is it that you want to say?' I asked him.

'There is something,' he said. 'You always knew me so well, Ethan.'

'Did I?' I was unaware that I possessed any insight into my father at all.

'Oh yes,' he said. 'You saw through me, boy. You always saw through me.'

He looked at me for a long time and I knew that it was true. I had never been taken in by his lies and sweet-talking as Cathy and my mother had.

'Say what you have to say and then leave us in peace,' I said.

My father took a deep breath and put his pale hands to his face. He kept them there for a moment before letting them slide slowly down. His eyes were closed, his mouth partly open.

'I want to tell a story –'

'A story?' I said. 'You've come back to tell us a story?'

'It's a story about me,' he said. 'It is my story.'

I was about to interrupt him again but something told me that we were destined to hear his tale and that to forestall it, therefore, was pointless and would only delay further our departure from this world.

'What do you say, Cathy?' I asked. 'Shall we hear his story?'

'Yes,' she said quietly.

THE MERMAID

I was not always an innkeeper. I was once a fisherman from a long line of fisherfolk. I had never wanted anything more than to go to sea with my father and my brothers.

I was the youngest of three brothers and no brothers ever loved each other more than we did. We looked out for one another at sea and on the shore, our own small nation, proud and fearless.

We were men, and when we came ashore we drank; but in those days I drank to be merry and nothing more. We drank in this very inn. They were happy times.

And being men, we naturally also competed for the attentions of the women hereabouts, though we never did so with any real animosity. No woman would ever mean more to us than we meant to each other. Or so we thought.

At the age of fourteen I fell for Catherine, the daughter of the innkeeper, though I don't think she saw me as anything but a boy then. In any event, she seemed besotted by a pale young son of the gentry who came to the inn from time to time, as rich young men will when they want to sow their wild oats. Thackeray, his name was – damn his eyes.

It pained my heart to see her take such an interest in that preening fop, but I was consoled soon enough by a chance encounter with another girl.

Agnes was a rare beauty and why she even noticed a boy like me I cannot say, but we seemed to form a bond instantly. She was the daughter of a local sailmaker. I went with my father to collect some new sails and there she was, her eyes shining like jewels.

While our fathers went about their business, we fell to talking and it felt so simple and easy. It was as if we had known each other for years. I forgot Catherine and Agnes filled that space like wine in an empty glass.

My father teased me when we left, but I could see that he was happy and regarded it as a good match – her father too.

A month or so later and the date for the wedding was set. Two happier people there could not have been in the entire world. If only I had known what a fragile thing that happiness was.

The man who saw Agnes fall said that she was walking along the cliff – a route we all took to the next bay – when a freak wind blew up such as he had never experienced. It came from nowhere and hit like a fist. He heard Agnes cry out as she stumbled, desperately trying to regain her balance, then tumbled over and fell to certain death on the rocks at the sea's edge below.

I say certain because that must surely have been her fate, though we never did recover her body. Her father and I walked the shore day after day for weeks. We sent word along the coast in either direction but there was no trace of her.

We could not bury what we could not find, but we did have a service of remembrance. Catherine came and she was, as she always was, a picture of kindness. But I was not to be mollified. My heart was raw.

I was determined that I should return to sea at

the first opportunity. My brothers tried to dissuade me, but I knew that I needed to get away from the daily reminders of my love and the sympathetic smiles of well-meaning townsfolk.

And so we sailed out into the wide Atlantic. When the land finally disappeared from sight, I did feel a little lighter in myself. The sea can do that for a man. The sea can heal just as it can kill.

We headed south towards the Bay of Biscay, and the weather could not have been in greater contrast to my state of mind. The sun shone and a fair breeze blew. Under different circumstances it would have been the perfect voyage and we would all have been in fine spirits.

But my father and brothers felt unable to enjoy this good fortune. If ever one of them broke out into laughter or singing as he went about his work, the others would look to me as though this behaviour would cause me some great affront. I assured them that I did not expect all to carry my burden of melancholy, but still the laughter died, the singing stopped.

And the cloud that covered me was soon mirrored in the heavens as sunshine gave way to a thick, grimy blanket of cloud. The breeze became a chill and gusting wind that snatched and tugged at the sails, and shoved us this way and that as we tried to control the bucking ship.

As if that were not enough, now – even though it was still only September – snowflakes began to be carried on the wind, just a few at first, but as the wind strengthened so their number increased until soon we were hardly able to see the other side of our fishing boat.

Our nets had been out when the wind struck and we struggled to haul them up. At least they seemed to be well filled. If we could get them aboard, we could try to ride the storm winds back home.

And so, slithering on the freezing deck and with the snow burning our hands, we heaved the nets towards the hold. As the fish tumbled into the darkness, we all saw the same thing and cried out in disbelief.

A woman had tumbled down along with the fish. She was naked, her long wet hair wrapped around her arms and breasts. I saw her face only for an instant, but it seared my eyes. She looked like Agnes.

My father was the first to come to his senses and he leapt down after the fish. We could barely see him in the hold, what with the darkness below and the snow swirling above.

Moments later, he was climbing out with the woman draped over his shoulder. My brothers rushed to his aid, but somehow I could not move. Her face was hidden now, buried in my father's shoulder, but the thought of Agnes had jumbled my senses.

They were about to be jumbled further, for as my father stepped on deck, it became clear that this was no ordinary woman. For where there should have been legs there was a long, scaled fish tail, finned and stripe-marked like a mackerel.

Jacob, my eldest brother, took her from my father and stood cradling her in his arms, one hand holding her naked waist, the other her shimmering tail.

'It's a mermaid!' he said in wonder, giving voice to all our thoughts. 'A real mermaid!'

'Is she alive?' asked Samuel, my other brother.

'Aye,' my father replied. 'She's still breathing. Just knocked unconscious, I reckon.'

'Should I throw her back, then, Father,' Jacob asked, 'or wait till she wakes?'

'Now hold on there,' said my father. 'Let's not be hasty. Do you remember the carnival that came to town last year? What might they pay for something like this, eh?'

'No!'

It was a few moments before I realised it was me who had shouted. All eyes turned to me.

'It's wrong!' I said. 'Have you not seen her face? She is the mirror of Agnes.'

'John,' said my father with a sad lilt to his voice, 'we feel your loss right keenly, you know that. But that thing is not Agnes, nor has nothing to do with her.'

'Some say mermaids are the souls of the drowned,' I said.

'Some say seals are souls of the drowned,' Jacob returned. 'People say all kinds of things.'

'Well,' I said, 'would you have believed in mermaids at all were you not holding one in your arms? Would any of you? We must put her back in the sea. We must!'

Samuel put his hand on my arm and I shrugged him away. He did it again and I pushed him. Samuel was quick-tempered at the best of times and pushed me back. I snatched a belaying pin and hit him hard around the side of the head.

My father rushed to his aid and they soon overpowered me as I threw punches at them in my efforts to get to Jacob, who still stood holding the sleeping mermaid. They eventually had no choice but to tie me to the foot of the mast, where I sat shouting and cursing while they did their best to ignore me and gathered instead around Jacob and the mermaid.

My father grabbed the creature by her hair and turned her head to face us. This increased my cries even more. The resemblance to Agnes was so marked I could not bear it.

And then, while we all watched, her eyes suddenly opened, making my siblings and my father jump. Then Jacob screamed.

It was hard to credit that he could make such a sound. Even from where I sat it was clear what had caused his distress: barbs had erupted from along the creature's length and pierced his arms and sides.

The mermaid opened her mouth and revealed a terrifying armoury of razor-sharp teeth. Then she turned to Jacob and, in one swift movement, ripped a hole in his throat, taking his windpipe and stifling his cry and his life. She fell from his arms and a second later Jacob tumbled to the deck after her, blood spouting from the wound.

The mermaid turned to my family, her face flecked with gore. She hissed and the colours of her scales flickered and moved up and down her body in waves.

Startled, my father leapt back and slipped on the

frozen deck. She was on him in an instant, her hands, which I now saw ended in talons, ripping at his clothes, her teeth seeking and finding flesh.

Samuel kicked the mermaid away and she slid across the deck, smacking against the bulwarks. He took his knife from its sheath and approached her as she lay, stunned, face down.

But it was a ruse. A flick of her tail sent the knife twirling through the air with such force that it embedded itself in the deck near my feet. Another flick of the spiked tail brought Samuel down and she fell on him, tearing and biting until there was no movement but hers.

She saw me and dragged herself across the deck. Oh – what a sight that was! Her face was dripping with blood, her bare body painted with it. When she got to within two or three feet of me, she stopped and stared, her head cocked to one side.

Was it Agnes? She looked so like her. Was it grief that made me see the similarity? God knows I wish I hadn't seen it. And did she remember me? She seemed to. At any rate, she left me and returned to my father and began, to my horror, to feed on what she had killed.

I shut my eyes to the sight but could not close my ears to the sound. I felt the snow on my face and prayed that she would finish me quickly.

Then I remembered the knife. I opened my eyes. Her back was turned to me. It was easy to grasp the hilt between my feet and pull it towards me.

I strained my fingers and grabbed the knife. There was only one great knot to cut out and I would be free. I went about my work as she fed.

All at once the ropes fell away and I was on my feet. I kicked the creature away from my father, momentarily frozen by the sight of the horror she had performed on his body.

'I'll kill you!' I yelled with tears in my eyes and grabbed the axe we kept by the mast for cutting the nets when they became entangled.

The mermaid turned to face me. Oh – she looked so much like Agnes that I could not move. But then she snarled and hissed and the spell was broken. I took her head off with one almighty blow and it thudded against the hatch cover. Her body flailed grotesquely for a few hideous moments.

I walked over to see the head and cried out in anguish as I saw poor Agnes looking back at me, as sweet as ever she was. Or so it seemed.

All this time the boat had been sailing blind, with no one to steer its course, and suddenly I heard a mighty rending noise as it struck a rock. I was knocked off my feet and I crashed on to my head. The last thing I recalled before I sank into unconsciousness was Agnes's head sliding past my eyes.

When I awoke I was on another ship – a larger vessel than my own. I wondered at first whether it might not be the fabled Black Ship that sailors speak of, but I was soon disabused of this notion. I was treated with great kindness and humour by all aboard. This was no ship of the dead. I had survived.

I could not speak of what had happened, save to say that I had lost my father and two brothers. I wondered how I could tell the tale and be believed. It was clear our ship had gone down before my rescuers arrived, taking all evidence of that creature with it. Everyone agreed it was a miracle that I was still alive.

I began to doubt what I had seen. Was it all devilry? I wondered. Or had I gone mad? That would certainly be what people at home would say if I tried to tell them. No – I decided to speak only of the shipwreck and my lucky escape.

I did not feel lucky though. Catherine's gentleman had incurred the wrath of his wealthy father for wooing an innkeeper's daughter and did not call on her as he had. I consoled her as a friend, but we soon became more than friends. She helped to calm my soul. And what she did not soothe, brandy did. It was then I became a drinker.

Catherine had been my first love and so I was overjoyed when she agreed to be my wife. If she noticed my drinking, she did not say. I think she thought to cure me of my sadness, and if any woman could have done so, it would have been her. But a madness had already taken root in me. My future was mapped. How I wish it might have been otherwise.

Cathy and I stared at my father as he once again bowed his head. When he finally looked back at us, I knew that he saw the coldness in my expression.

'So – no forgiveness from you, then, Ethan?' he asked.

'I feel sorry for the life Fate handed you, Father,' I said. 'And sorry, too, for Agnes and for your brothers and father and the terrible way they died ...'

'But?'

'But I do not see that any of that meant you had to murder us, your children.'

'My mind was damaged, Ethan,' he said. 'I didn't know what I was doing.' Our father clenched his eyes shut and shook his head mournfully. But I could feel no sympathy for him.

'And what about you, Cathy?' he said when he opened his eyes once more.

Cathy made no reply, but turned her face away.

'Let me stay,' he said. 'I know how you like stories. I could tell you tales of the inmates at the asylum. We had a boy there who had a terrible fear of railway tunnels. He kept crying out about a woman dressed in white who –'

'No,' I said. 'Cathy and I wish to be left in peace.'

My father nodded. A tear trickled down his face. He looked from me to Cathy and back to me, and then slowly he became more and more indistinct until finally all was shadow once again.

'Father?' said Cathy quietly.

'He's gone,' I said, 'and shan't return. Let's sleep now, Cathy.'

'Can I stay beside you?' she asked.

'Of course.'

And we embraced while snow fell more heavily through the holes in the ceiling. Soon we closed our eyes and drifted into the blackness like snowflakes, joining together with others like us who were floating through darkness to land on a vast black ocean.